蕭仁徵
現代畫開拓展

墨動

Ink Movement
**Hsiao Jen-cheng and the Expansion
of Modern Painting**

國立歷史博物館
National Museum of History

國立臺灣師範大學美術學系

目錄
CONTENTS

◆ **序文** Prefaces

**資深藝術家蕭仁徵在戰後臺灣美術現代畫
運動中的「在地現代化」實驗**／廖新田 ····················· 4
Hsiao Jen-cheng's "Local Modernization" Experiment and the
Contemporary Painting Movement in Taiwan:
In Lieu of a Preface / Liao Hsin-tien

國家桂冠‧藝苑經典──「蕭仁徵現代畫開拓展」／白適銘 ··· 8
A National Laureate and Artistic Paradigm: Preface to "Ink Movement:
Hsiao Jen-cheng and the Expansion of Modern Painting" / Pai Shi-min

我的展覽‧我的畫／蕭仁徵 ····························· 11
My Exhibition, My Paintings / Hsiao Jen-cheng

◆ **專文** Essay

抽象的抒情：蕭仁徵的筆墨山水／邱琳婷 ··················· 15
Abstract Lyricism: Hsiao Jen-cheng's Ink Brush Landscapes / Chiu Ling-ting

◆ **圖版** Plates

風景中的詩意 ······································· 22
Poetic Expression in Landscape Painting

直覺性的創造 ······································· 58
Intuitive Art

筆墨自由及其他 ····································· 110
Liberation of Brushwork and Other Forms

◆ **附錄** Appendix

蕭仁徵創作年表 ····································· 138
Chronology

資深藝術家蕭仁徵在戰後臺灣美術現代畫運動中的「在地現代化」實驗

認識蕭仁徵（1925-）前輩，我的內心有一份深深的虧欠。國立歷史博物館（以下簡稱史博館）需要閉館整建好幾年之際，接獲蕭老師來電，表明已審查通過展覽申請。他因為年事已高，表示是否能儘早安排展覽以完成心願。我們類似這樣的案子已累積達三四十位，即使將他放在第一位也要幾年之後的事，實在是緩不濟急。我即刻帶領史博館一行人前往基隆蕭宅拜訪，了解狀況。蕭老師精神仍奕奕，對藝術充滿創作的熱情。夫人詹碧琴（1944-）女士其實是水墨大師傅狷夫的少數女弟子之一。伉儷相互扶持，傳為藝壇佳話。

蕭老和臺灣藝壇、特別是史博館的緣分很早。1960 年，第一屆長風畫展參展者為趙淑敏、蕭仁徵、鄭世鈺、祝頌康、吳兆賢、蔡崇武、張熾昌、吳鼎藩等八位。1961 年史博館徵集作品，他的兩張水彩畫《災難》、《哀鳴》和劉國松、胡奇中、韓湘寧、顧福生各四件油畫，陳庭詩、李錫奇各三件版畫一起被選送參加第六屆巴西聖保羅雙年展。1972 年中華民國水墨畫會會員作品水墨畫聯展於史博館國家畫廊舉行；1973 年臺灣水彩畫會會員十人聯合畫展也在國家畫廊展出，展出名單中皆有他的名字，可見，他相當活躍於當時的藝術活動。隔年，他和王藍、何懷碩、舒曾祉、席德進、高山嵐、張杰、藍清輝、劉其偉、龍思良一起在省立博物館（今國立臺灣博物館）舉行水彩聯展。也是這一年，水墨畫聯展在史博館畫廊舉行，他和劉國松、文霽、馮鍾睿、楚山青、劉墉等人一同展出。藝術評論名家姚夢谷先生曾經如此賞析他的創作：

> 活潑中顯示安定與沉著，筆觸靈活，富於感情，造形別具匠心。

1975 年，一位他的藝術「粉絲」，居住在今新北市的林義祥投書《雄獅美術》49 期，認為蕭仁徵的水墨風格特殊，希望能多多介紹他的作品：

> 我曾經在一次水墨畫聯展裏發現蕭仁徵的水墨畫，那樣寧靜的墨，那樣詩情的意境，那樣超脫的感覺，使我真正感到一股水墨的味道：不是傳統發霉的墨也不是現代人製造的怪異芳味的墨。這位曾經在歷史博物館開過個展、入選巴黎美展、聖保羅國際雙年展的水墨畫家，雄獅美術似乎未介紹過他的作品。我想或許出刊了香港水墨畫家作品之後，陸續的，我們可以詳盡介紹臺灣的水墨畫家。

這年，中國水墨畫會十四人聯展也有他的身影，又是在史博館展出。1978 年，藝術家畫廊舉行會員聯展，他和朱為白、顧重光、林燕、文霽、楚戈、梁奕焚、楊熾宏、江漢東、董振平、席德進、吳學讓、陳庭詩、李錫奇、吳昊等共同展出。名家現代雕塑展也有蕭仁徵的出品。1979 年美國在臺協會文化中心臺北處舉行其個展。1984 年中國現代水墨畫學會慶祝雙十國慶六十人聯展，他也是其中之一。羅青曾將他歸類為「過渡期第二代的畫家」。他也自詡自己的創作是「新時代中的新關係」，這可以從他和王爾昌、文霽曾以「新國畫展」命名展覽名稱看出（1989 年於黎明藝文中心）。1995 年，二十一世紀現代水墨畫會成立，已屆從心之年的他也是四十位會員之一。

以上有些過於細瑣的描述，無非是為了證明蕭仁徵是臺灣現代水墨的耕耘前輩，深深鑲嵌在臺灣現代水墨的網絡之中，是我們珍貴的文化資產。過去的辛勤痕跡，吾輩豈可遺珠？回到開頭的虧欠，如何能稍稍彌補不能立刻展出的缺憾呢？史博館實踐了文化部重建臺灣藝術史的精神，因此我們先從建構蕭老前輩的檔案、文獻、作品整理開始並進行研究，於是有 2020 年底《畫是想出來畫 想是畫出來的—蕭仁徵傳記暨檔案彙編》的出版，希望能為臺灣美術史增添些新材料。

　　史博館正在如火如荼地閉館整建當中，但仍然秉持「修館不休館，服務不打烊」的精神，乃決定在國立臺灣師範大學（以下簡稱師大）德群畫廊展出蕭老前輩的回顧展。師大美術系是臺灣美術發展的重要基地，相得益彰。由於蕭老師非常希望能在史博館國家畫廊展出，我們乃創意發想，將原先二樓「國家畫廊」的匾額暫時移過來掛置，象徵：國立歷史博物館所到之處就有史博館的身影。場所的意義是精神性的、象徵性的，如同藝術與文化的核心價值。感謝師大美術系白適銘主任排除萬難讓這個展覽得以順利進行，更感謝蕭仁徵前輩對臺灣美術的貢獻，並諒解這次的權宜性安排。

國立歷史博物館 館長

Hsiao Jen-cheng's "Local Modernization" Experiment and the Contemporary Painting Movement in Taiwan: In Lieu of a Preface

Getting to know Master Hsiao Jen-cheng (1925-) has sowed a deep sense of indebtedness in me. On the eve of the National Museum of History's (NMH) closure for renovations, I received his phone call. In our conversation he told me that his exhibition application had been approved and, being a man of advanced years, he hoped for a swift process to fulfill his wishes. As there were already about 30 or 40 similar exhibition projects on the docket, even if we prioritized his exhibition, it would still be several years before it could actually take place. Together with museum staff, I immediately arranged a visit to Mr. Hsiao's residence in Keelung. Master Hsiao, while advanced in physical years, is still energetic and full of passion toward art. This passion is shared by his wife, Chan Pi-chin (1944-), who was one of the few female disciples of master ink painter Fu Chuan-fu. Their support for each other in both art and life sets a heartwarming example for the art world.

Rather early in his career, Master Hsiao established a connection to Taiwan's art scene and especially to the NMH. He presented his work in the first Chang Feng Painting Exhibition with seven other participants: Chao Shu-min, Cheng Shi-yu, Chu Song-kang, Wu Chao-hsien, Tsai Chong-wu, Chang Zhi-chang, and Wu Ding-fan. In 1961, the NMH selected two of his watercolors, *Disaster and Wail*, for the sixth Sao Paulo Art Biennial in Brazil, along with four oil paintings each by Liu Kuo-sung, Hu Chi, Han Hsiang-ning, and Ku Fu-sheng, and three prints each by Chen Ting-shih and Li Shi-chi. In 1972, a joint exhibition of the members of the ROC Ink Wash Painting Society took place in the NMH's National Gallery. The next year, a joint exhibition of 10 members of the Taiwan Watercolor Painting Association was held in the same space. Hsiao participated in both exhibitions, indicating his active presence in the art world at the time. The next year, he joined forces with Wang Lan, Ho Huai-shuo, Shu Zeng-Zhi, Shiy De jinn, Kao San-lan, Chang Chieh, Lan Ching-hui, Max Liu, and Long Sih-liang to hold a joint exhibition of watercolor painting in the Taiwan Provincial Museum (today's National Taiwan Museum). That same year, he presented his ink-wash paintings in an NMH exhibition that also included works by Liu Kuo-sung, Wen Chi, Feng Jung-ruei, Chu Shan-ching, and Liu Yong. In 1975, *Lion Art Monthly*, No. 49, published a "fan letter" by one Mr. Lin Yi-hsiang. In the letter, Lin felt that Master Hsiao's ink painting had a unique style and hoped that the publication could offer more insights into his work:

> I discovered Hsiao Jen-cheng's ink-wash paintings in a joint exhibition. His work, with serene ink, poetic stances, and transcendental sensations, have truly helped me understand ink painting. It is not the antique ink style nor the artificial and weird taste of modern painting. This painter has held a solo exhibition in the NMH and was selected by the Paris Exhibition and the Sao Paolo Biennial, but *Lion Art Monthly* has never discussed his work. I suggest that, after the articles about ink painters in Hong Kong, maybe it's time to offer a detailed introduction of the ink painters of Taiwan.

In 1975, Master Hsiao participated in a joint exhibition with 14 members of the Chinese Ink Painting Association, again at the NMH. In 1978, the "Artists' Gallery" organized a joint exhibition of members, showing works by Master Hsiao along with Chu Wei-bor, Ku Chung Kuang, Lin Yen, Wen Chi, Chu Ko, Liang Yi-fen, Yang Chi-hung, Chiang Han-tong, Dong Jhen-ping, Shiy De jinn, Wu

Hsueh-jang, Chen Ting-shih, Li Shi-chi, and Wu Hao. He also presented work in a modern sculpture exhibition by famous artists. The year after he even held a solo exhibition in the Taipei Office of the American Institute in Taiwan. In 1984, the Chinese Modern Ink Painting Association celebrated Double Ten National Day by organizing a joint exhibition of 60 artists, Hsiao among them.

Luo Ching used to categorize Master Hsiao as "the second-generation painter of the interim phase." Master Hsiao himself also believed that his works represented "new relations of the new age," indicated by the title of his joint exhibition with Wang Erh-chang and Wen Chi, "Exhibition of New National Painting" (1989, Lee-ming Arts and Cultural Center). In 1995, the 21st Century Modern Ink Painting Society was founded, counting the septuagenarian among its 40 founding members.

The overdetailed description above is meant to prove that Hsiao Jen-cheng is a hardworking progenitor of modern ink painting in Taiwan. His contributions are deeply intertwined with the movement, making him a precious cultural asset. We should not forget the traces of his artistic lineage.

As for Master Hsiao's hope expressed in the beginning of this article, we thought long and hard for a way to remedy the delay in holding this exhibition. As the museum accords with the Ministry of Culture's agenda of rebuilding Taiwanese art history, we began by building an archive of Master Hsiao's work and life. The result of this effort, a publication titled *Painting is from Thinking, and Thinking is from Painting: Hsiao, Jen-cheng's Biography and Archive*, aims to provide new resources for studying Taiwan's art history.

The NMH renovation project is currently in full swing, but, under our slogan "shuttered, but not closed," we have arranged to hold a retrospective exhibition for Master Hsiao in the Teh Chun Gallery of National Taiwan Normal University (NTNU). As the Department of Fine Arts at NTNU is a vital hub for art in Taiwan, there is no more appropriate venue for presenting Master Hsiao's achievements. As Master Hsiao deeply wishes to present his works in the National Gallery of NMH, we figured out a creative solution: We symbolically moved the plaque for the gallery to NTNU. The presence of the museum naturally hinges on its active engagement in the promotion of art, as art and culture are our core values.

I want to express my appreciation to Professor Pai Shih-min, chair of the Department of Fine Arts at NTNU. He has devoted himself and overcome many difficulties to facilitate the successful organization of this exhibition. I also want to thank Master Hsiao for his enormous contributions to Taiwanese art and for his understanding of this expedient arrangement.

Director-General, National Museum of History

國家桂冠・藝苑經典──「蕭仁徵現代畫開拓展」序

　　新冠肺炎疫情仍四處肆虐之現今，臺灣防疫體系因控制得宜，社會整體遭受較少衝擊，國內藝文活動亦能有限開放，透過網絡通路或實體設施，展現世界上難得一見的活絡光景。今年五月，變種病毒入侵臺灣前夕，臺師大藝術學院與國立歷史博物館簽訂合作意向書，未來並希望朝「策略聯盟」之路徑邁進，共同推動臺灣美術史百年重建之歷史志業。

　　早此之前，今年三月之初，臺師大美術系即率先與史博館商議，由本人與廖新田館長進行初步溝通，合意於本系德群畫廊以「國家畫廊」之名義舉辦邀請展出，作為史博館修館期間二館間最早之合作範例，創造官、學、藝「三贏」契機，此即本展成立之由來。同時，由於此種特殊館際合作、移動借展模式，開啟與網路虛擬世界不同之「有形」博物館模式，更成為國內稀有之先例。

　　極其幸運地，歷經五月中旬以來疫情波瀾起伏之震盪與驚惶，拜管制逐漸解封或降級之賜，自十一月初起為期四週，規劃多時之本展將在此「雙館合一」的形式下隆重開幕。本人作為臺師大美術系之現任主管代表，誠摯歡迎各位貴賓之蒞臨，共同見證二館通力合作之歷史創舉，為已屆九十七高齡、臺灣現代水墨先行者蕭仁徵老師舉辦個展，深感榮耀與責任重大，同時感謝廖館長的遠見、魄力及完善擘劃。

　　本展覽以「墨動─蕭仁徵現代畫開拓展」為題，展現藝術家自1958年迄今逾一甲子之久的豐碩創作軌跡，百餘件不同時期之作品，包含水墨、彩墨、複合媒材、書法、抽象書藝、水彩等多元面向，不僅具體反映前衛、實驗及批判傳統之現代改革精神，並突顯戰後威權體制下藝術家孤獨卻自足的個人處境。透過數十年有關「改革筆墨」、「創造形式」及「探索結構」等抽象繪畫純粹性、精神性之推敲琢磨，蕭仁徵現代藝術拓荒之路，已然走出寬闊而自由的通衢大道。

　　不論是自嚼孤獨、思鄉情切，抑或是盤桓山水、遊藝筆端，這些造型抽象卻色彩豐富、線條優美的符號、筆觸、色塊或墨跡，或諧擬，或無語，或靈動，或虛靜，皆以極其鮮活、瀟灑而沁人心脾的姿態，共同營造遠離濁世、天籟繞樑般的淨土世界。九十餘載的青春歲月中，三分之二浸染奉獻於此，幾與民國同壽的蕭仁徵的世紀開拓，已成為百年國畫改革史中的國家桂冠，而其藝術成就更可謂斯界經典，藉由本展覽期導引觀眾進入這段輝煌歷史，並分享其最直率、純真而無畏無懼的藝旅壯遊生涯。謹此敬頌展覽順利成功！

國立臺灣師範大學美術系系主任

白適銘

A National Laureate and Artistic Paradigm: Preface to "Ink Movement: Hsiao Jen-cheng and the Expansion of Modern Painting"

As COVID-19 wreaks havoc throughout the world, Taiwan has been an exemplar of appropriate pandemic response, allowing society to escape its worst effects. People can still enjoy access to art and cultural activities — albeit somewhat limited — both online and in person, expressing an enthusiastic energy rarely seen in today's world. This May, just before the first major domestic outbreak of COVID-19, the College of Arts at National Taiwan Normal University (NTNU) signed a memorandum of understanding with the National Museum of History (NMH) to forge a "strategic alliance" with the goal of reconstructing Taiwan's art history.

Earlier this year in March, the Department of Fine Arts at NTNU and NMH opened a discussion about possible cooperation, resulting in an agreement with NMH Director Liao Hsin-tien to organize "National Gallery" exhibitions in the department's Teh Chun Gallery. This collaboration while the museum is undergoing renovations creates a win-win-win situation for the government, academia, and artists, and sets the stage for this exhibition. At the same time, this unique model of inter-institutional cooperation presents a tangible rather than virtual option for collaborative exhibitions, setting a rare precedent in Taiwan.

Fortunately, the turbulence brought by the outbreak has subsided and measures have eased, allowing this "two-in-one" exhibition to open for four weeks beginning in early November. As representative of the Department of Fine Arts, I sincerely welcome you to witness this historical collaboration. I feel deeply the honor and pressure involved in preparing this solo exhibition for master Hsiao Jen-cheng, Taiwan's 97-year-old pioneer of modern ink painting. I would also like to thank Director Liao for his vision, audacity, and thoughtful planning.

This exhibition, titled "Ink Movement: Hsiao Jen-cheng and the Expansion of Modern Painting," showcases more than 100 of Hsiao's creations since 1958, covering different phases and diverse media such as ink-wash painting, ink-and-color painting, multimedia, traditional and abstract calligraphy, and watercolor. These works substantialize the reforming spirit of modernity through the avant-garde, the experimental, and critique of tradition. They also highlight the personal stance of a lonely yet self-sufficient artist working under the authoritarian post-war system. After reflecting on and struggling with concepts of brushwork reformation, form, and structure for decades, Hsiao has mapped out a broad and flexible space for himself within modern art.

In his work are figures formed by beautiful lines, brushstrokes, color blocks, or ink traces. They convey senses of solitude or nostalgia, of sojourning in mountains and rivers, or pleasurable play of brushwork. They create serene and paradisal worlds with refreshing styles of parody, wordlessness, inspiration, or void. Hsiao has spent more than two-thirds of his more than nine decades of life creating art, making him a national laureate whose achievements set a paradigm for art situated within history. I hope this exhibition can bring viewers into this splendid past, led in this grand tour by a straightforward, pure, and fearless artist. It is my sincerest wish that this exhibition find success.

Chair, Department of Fine Arts, NTNU

Pai Shi-min

我的展覽・我的畫

我接到國立歷史博物館來函是民國 105 年 6 月 29 日的事，時年正值 90 歲。史博館同意邀請我展出，展覽之檔期另行通知，但又逢史博館大修建，要在史博館展出，恐怕尚有年月。

很幸運，2020 年 4 月間，國立歷史博物館館長廖新田先生仁心義舉，時不容緩地來電與我聯絡，並同展覽組 4、5 人駕臨寒舍敘談。館長告知我擬借用師範大學德群畫廊展覽。

德群藝廊是為了紀念朱德群先生在國際藝壇的榮耀而設立，朱先生原為臺灣師範學院藝術系教授，後留學法國，為法蘭西藝術院中的第一位華裔院士，藝術地位高超，再加上館長言，已與師大美術系主任白適銘教授研議妥善，再加上：「朱德群教授又是你的老師」，我便很高興地接受了。

時於民國 39 年間，其時擔任中國美術協會會長是胡偉克先生，朱德群教授在中國美術協會研究班任課，我選他的素描課。這段真實有年的師生因緣，就是這樣的。

我幼年即喜愛繪畫，每到年盡的除夕時，四伯父就在廳堂的壁上掛些字畫，我很喜歡閱覽。有一次新年的正月，隨著母親去他堂妹家，便看到壁間掛滿字畫，其中有一幅紅梅中堂畫，我很喜愛，回家即畫了一小幅。讀小學常看教美術課的鞏老師畫的梅花，來台任教時也常畫梅花。

我從事繪畫沒有拜過師，常醉心於繪事，也常常逛書店、走馬路，翻閱有書畫的雜誌，往往為了一張喜愛的畫，將整本就買回了。

我喜歡閱覽繪畫，不愛臨摹他人的畫作，至今數十年來只臨摹過八大山人的小幅花鳥畫，石濤的山水圖而已，但常赴故宮博物院閱覽前人書畫。

水彩畫我也很喜歡，其原因是來臺時，畫水墨畫不易找工作，後來便自學水彩畫。在學校任教時，一日閱報，有美國十大水彩畫家之一曾景文先生在台北西寧南路記者之家展覽最後一日，我冒著颱風，於民國 42 年 10 月 9 日下午前往參觀，回基隆時颱風已很厲害了，可說我對水彩的喜愛是風雨無阻。

此時，我畫水彩、水墨畫，由半抽象至全抽象，其水墨抽象畫極少發表，水彩抽象畫，則常代表國家參加歐、美、日、俄、紐西蘭、西班牙等國際展覽。日、英、美及國內重要美術館也典藏我的水墨、水彩畫作品。

其次，關於我參加第 6 屆巴西聖保羅國際展覽的畫作「哀鳴」，是我自藏的作品，我愛鴿子、養鴿子、畫鴿子，鴿子，就是人稱的和平鴿。我愛世人和平相處，而畫和平鴿「尋求」一件，「渴望」二件，「哀鳴」三件，和平鴿最後卻等不到真和平，只能發出哀鳴！！！

最後，謝謝廖館長與國立師範大學美術系系主任白適銘教授，熱心策畫，使我的展覽能順利展出。

My Exhibition, My Paintings

t was on June 29, 2016, when I was already 90 years old, that I received a letter from the National Museum of History inviting me to hold an exhibition at an undecided future date. The invitation came just as the museum was preparing to close for renovations, so I didn't know how long I had to wait to present my work.

Fortunately, four years later in April 2020, the museum's kind and enthusiastic director Liao Hsin-tien contacted me. He visited my home with four or five staff members to tell me about plans to hold an exhibition of my work at the Teh Chun Gallery at National Taiwan Normal University (NTNU).

The Teh Chun Gallery was created to celebrate Chu Teh-chun's incredible artistic achievements. Mr. Chu was originally a professor in the Department of Fine Arts at NTNU before pursuing further study in France, where he became the first ethnic Chinese member of the Académie des Beaux-Arts and enjoyed the elevated status that came with it. He also happened to be my former teacher. Reminding me of this, Director Liao told me that he had already made arrangements with the current department chair, Professor Pai Shih-min, to hold an exhibition in the gallery. I enthusiastically accepted his offer.

Our teacher-disciple relationship, authentic and long past, began like this: It was around 1950 and Hu Wei-ke was president of the Art Association of the Republic of China. At that time, Professor Chu was teaching for the association, and I took his drawing class.

I have loved painting since I was young. Every year on Lunar New Year's Eve, I would look forward to seeing the paintings and calligraphy my fourth uncle would display in his entry hall. One time, during the first month of the new year, I went with my mother to visit her cousin's house with its many pieces hanging from the walls. One painting of red plum flowers especially caught my eye, inspiring me to try to replicate it as soon as we got home. In my elementary school days, I often admired the plum flowers painted by my art teacher, Mr. Gong. Even later when I started teaching in Taiwan, I kept painting plum flowers.

Painting for me was an indulgence. I never studied with any teacher, but often visited bookstores and perused magazines with photographs of painting and calligraphy. I would sometimes purchase them, even if each only had one painting that I liked.

I like to view paintings, but I don't like to copy or emulate others' work. Over these decades, I mostly just copied small flower-and-bird paintings by Bada Shanren and landscapes by Shi Tao. I also loved to visit the National Palace Museum and appreciate ancient masterpieces.

When I first came to Taiwan, it was difficult to find a job with ink painting skills, so I decided to teach myself watercolor painting and came to love the form. One day when I was still teaching, I read in a newspaper that Mr. Tseng Jing-wen, praised as one of the 10 best watercolor painters in the USA, was exhibiting his works in the Journalist's House on Xining South Road in Taipei. Since it was already the last day of the show, I braved a typhoon to see it in the afternoon of October 9, 1953. The storm was raging terribly when I returned to Keelung, but it was not enough to stop my love of watercolor.

At that time, I used both watercolor and ink to create semi-abstract and abstract paintings. I rarely showed my abstract ink paintings, but my watercolors were often selected by the government to show in exhibitions in Europe, the USA, Japan, Russia, New Zealand, and Spain. My works have also been collected by major museums in Japan, the UK, the USA, and Taiwan.

I next want to talk about my painting *Wail*, which was selected for the Sixth Sao Paulo Art Biennial in Brazil. This work, which remains in my personal collection, features a subject that I love to both keep and paint. These are the so-called doves of peace, representing a quality I love to see in the world. I have many paintings of doves, including one titled *Search*, two titled *Desire*, and three titled *Wailing*. In the end, doves can never meet real peace, but are consigned to futilely wail in misery. What a tragedy!

Finally, I want to thank Director Liao and Professor Pai. It was through their enthusiasm and organization that this exhibition became a reality.

Hsiao Jen-cheng

專文
Essay

「惟轉化為文字，為形象，為音符，為節奏，
可望將生命某一種形式，某一種狀態，凝固下來」
—1961 沈從文，〈抽象的抒情〉

*"Only through a transformation into words, images, music notes,
or rhythms can one solidify certain form or conditions of life."*
Shen Cong-wen, "Abstract Lyricism," 1961

抽象的抒情：蕭仁徵的筆墨山水 [1]

■邱琳婷
輔仁大學文創學程兼任助理教授

起初這世界曾是新鮮的。人一開口說話就如詩詠。爲外界事物命名每成靈感：妙喻奇譬脫口而出，如自然從感官流露出來的東西。[2]

C. Day Lewis (1904-1972), The Poetic Image

一、前言

1950 年代的臺灣畫壇，興起了一股水墨現代化的浪潮，「五月畫會」和「東方畫會」即是大家所熟知的代表。影響這兩個畫會的李仲生，他對「現代繪畫」的思考，則將中國國劇、書法、金石等創作特徵，與西方達達派以後的前衛繪畫相比擬。[3]「五月畫會」的劉國松，受到其啟發所創作的抽象水墨，即明顯地承載著中國文藝的抒情傳統之特質。

相較於學院派的畫家而言，自學出身的蕭仁徵，於此時期所創作的抽象畫，則提供我們一個更直接且樸實的視角，思考藝術創作中抒情傳統之源頭。換句話說，蕭仁徵如何透過自己的生活經驗進行創作，或可讓我們更直接地回探人與景物相遇之初的感動與紀錄。

二、風景中的詩意

蕭仁徵 1958 年所繪的《雨中樹》（圖 1），曾於 1959 年入選法國巴黎國際雙年展，並於當地展出。他回憶創作此畫時提到：

畫之前呢，也許可以有一種想法、觀察，我畫這張畫的時候，我是坐在那邊，面對著風景，仔細觀察下雨中的樹，並逐漸有了感覺和想法。就是說，我怎麼樣把面前的風景，能變成不一樣，而且還需要有一種詩意的感覺。有這樣想法後，才會有那樣的描繪，也才會有那樣的感覺。[4]

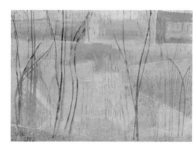

圖 1　雨中樹

圖 2　灰色的樹 (1911)
By Piet Mondrian - www.gemeentemuseum.nl：Home：Info：Pic, Public Domain, https://commons.wikimedia.org/w/index.php?curid=37613979

1　本文原以〈抽象的抒情：蕭仁徵的繪畫觀〉為題，刊載於《畫是想出來畫想是畫出來的—蕭仁徵傳記暨檔案彙編》（台北：國立歷史博物館，2020），頁 18-24；今增補「筆墨的自由度」一節，並將副標題改為蕭仁徵的筆墨山水。

2　C. Day Lewis, The Poetic Image, 轉引自陳世驤作、王靖獻譯，〈原興：兼論中國文學特質〉，《中國文化研究所學報》，第 3 卷第 1 期（1970.9），頁 151。

3　邱琳婷，《臺灣美術史》（台北：五南出版社，2019，三刷），頁 355。

4　邱琳婷，〈蕭仁徵訪問稿〉，2020.6.11。

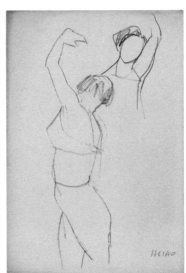

圖 3　舞者 (1)、(2)、(3)

　　這件作品，以線條及塊面所組成的構圖元素，雖與西方畫家蒙德里安（Piet Cornelies Mondrian，1872-1944）1911 年的《灰色的樹》（圖 2）近似，但兩人賦予線條與塊面的質感，卻顯得十分迥異。不同於蒙德里安以「精簡」的原則，不斷消除畫家認為畫面上多餘存在的線條，進而達到純粹化的「抽象」特質；蕭仁徵的《雨中樹》則以姿態各異的線條與濃淡相間的色調，流淌出一股「詩意」的氛圍。畫面中時而連續、時而間斷的點與線，不禁令人聯想起唐代詩人李白《琵琶行》中的一段詩句：

　　大絃嘈嘈如急雨，小絃切切如私語。

　　嘈嘈切切錯雜彈，大珠小珠落玉盤。

　　蕭仁徵雖然沒有明言畫面中構圖元素的所指為何？但在將此畫與李白此詩相對照之後，我們卻發現「詩」與「畫」之間驚人的吻合；即《雨中樹》中似樹幹的線條宛如嘈嘈的大絃，而畫中的短線則似切切的小絃，兩者共同演譯出「嘈嘈切切錯雜彈，大珠小珠落玉盤」的印象。此作可視為現代抽象畫，如何反映抒情傳統的一個佳例。

　　再者，《詩經》中運用的「興」（起興），可說是抒情傳統最早的創作方法。陳世驤考證「興」的字源時，提出此字在甲骨文中的象形意義，乃是指「四手合扛一物」之象；而在鐘鼎文裡，因增加了「口」之故，而延申有「群眾舉物發聲」；若再強調了「旋轉」現象，則逐漸發展為「群眾不僅平舉一物，尚能旋游」的「舞蛹」之意。換句話說，陳世驤總結道：「『興』乃是初民合群舉物旋游時所發出的聲音，帶著神采飛逸，共同舉起一件物體而旋轉。」[5] 此段對《詩經》原始創作情感的探求，乃是為了揭示紀錄各地生活經驗的《詩經・國風》，所流露出的個人情感，實反映出「抒情詩」的真義。[6] 而蕭仁徵以簡筆速寫三名舞者旋轉姿態的小品《三個舞者》（圖 3），則清楚地以圖像闡釋「興」的思維。

5　陳世驤，前引文，頁 144 － 145。

6　同前註，頁 145。

圖4　三人芭蕾　圖爲1926年「三人芭蕾」在柏林演出時所拍攝的服裝照片。　　圖5　哀鳴
（圖片提供：原點出版《包浩斯關鍵故事100》，頁198）。

　　蕭仁徵曾提到自己對於現代繪畫的吸收，主要來自1950、60年代，他逛台北書店（三省書店、鴻儒堂等）或書攤所販賣的畫冊和雜誌，得到的靈感。[7]因此，蕭仁徵1960年所繪《三個舞者》一作，令筆者不禁想起包浩斯中史雷梅爾（Oskar Schlemmer，1888-1943）的作品《三人芭蕾》（圖4）。創作者如此闡釋：「舞碼的概念源自於三和弦＝三音調的和弦，這齣芭蕾是三的舞蹈。它由三名舞者演出，分成三部分，每一部分都由一個不同的顏色主導：黃色、粉紅色和黑色，每個顏色都會誘發不同的情緒，從幽默進展到嚴肅。」[8]

三、直覺性的創造

不受學院技巧與師承束縛的蕭仁徵，如此自剖其創作歷程：

> 我回憶自己繪製作品的過程，這也不是說胸有成竹，或有一個模樣，完全不是！只有一個想法，就是要表現某一種畫的一個想法，或將一個人物的樣子畫出來，這是第一個。第二個呢，就是我不知道要畫什麼，但是我畫筆一下去，兩、三筆以後，我就知道我要畫什麼，這是我做抽象畫的一個性格。[9]

　　從這段自述可知，蕭仁徵對於視覺之美的追求，乃是在創作的過程中逐漸完成的。一般論及美與藝術的相關著作，主要圍繞在人類對於美和藝術的感應，也即是所謂的「美感經驗」。而此種用來形容「無以名之的種種心情、經驗以及對藝術和美的情緒感應」，也往往與美的認知（cognitio aesthetica）、凝神專注（concentration）、著迷（enchantment）、靈魂的內感（sensus animi）等概念有關。[10]高友工在談論「美感經驗」時，曾提出「直覺性的創造」一詞，用來說明擴展經驗與感受的方式。他如此解釋：「…創作過程常被視爲一個美感經驗的起點。這也可以說對這些創造者，技巧問題已不再干擾他們的創造活動，而這活動自可溶入一個經驗內省的過程中。…對他們來說，也可以說這整個美感經驗即是一種生活經驗，反映了生命活動的眞諦。

7　邱琳婷，〈蕭仁徵訪問稿〉，2020.6.11。

8　Frances Ambler 著，吳莉君譯，《包浩斯關鍵故事100》（台北：原點出版，2019），頁199。

9　邱琳婷，〈蕭仁徵訪問稿〉，2020.6.11。

10　Wtadystaw Tatarkiewicz 著，劉文潭譯，《西洋六大學理念史》（台北：聯經出版社，1989），頁383-390。

圖6　飢餓者

圖7　賽犬

創造的目的不是在藝術，而是在其經驗本身⋯」[11]

　　的確，蕭仁徵的創作觀，清楚地反映了「美感經驗即是一種生活經驗」。1961年的《哀鳴》（圖5），即是紀錄一段蕭仁徵難忘的生活經驗。他回憶到：

　　我服務的學校有一年遇到颱風，有隻鴿子飛到學校裡，我有一個學生看到了，他跟我說，於是我買了籠子，將牠放在裡面，每次下課的時候，我就看一看這隻鴿子。有時我想讓牠活動一下，就將教室窗子都關起來，但牠都站著不飛，只是伸伸翅膀。有一天，有一個朋友來了，他說老師你這鴿子關太久了，或許可以讓牠自由。他的話提醒了我，我就把牠放出來，鴿子飛到旁邊，停在那裡展開翅膀，後來有一群鴿子從屋頂經過，牠也就跟著飛起來，但那群鴿子飛得太急了，第二天，我學生說鴿子已死掉了，⋯那隻鴿子已經不在了，但我每一次下課回來，心裡面總會想到這隻鴿子，鴿子死掉了，心裡面也不快樂，於是產生這一張，半抽象的。[12]

　　至於1959年的《飢餓者》（圖6）一作，則是蕭仁徵對生活周遭所見流浪漢的描繪：

　　⋯事前也可能沒有什麼想法，畫的過程才出現一種想法，它叫《飢餓者》。這就好像是一個窮苦的人沒有飯吃，如流浪漢，或無家可歸的人，而且居無定所，住的地方也沒有。我想以一個病人的樣子來建構這街頭全無生意的感覺。[13]

　　其實，這件看似靜物畫（西瓜）的作品，若非參照畫家的講解，很難將其與人物畫聯想在一起。蕭仁徵從「食物」（如其所言「這就好像是一個窮苦的人沒有飯吃」）到「人物」（如他說「以一個病人的樣子來建構這街頭全無生意的感覺」）的思維過程，透露出他對弱勢者基本生活需求匱乏的感觸。

　　再者，1965年的《賽犬》（圖7），描繪的是一場親眼所見的賽事。蕭仁徵如此道：

　　這是我在學校服務時，我的班級在二樓，朝著外面大操場看基隆市的大操場，有一年臺灣

11　高友工，《中國美典與文學研究論集》（台北：國立臺灣大學，2011），頁48。

12　邱琳婷，〈蕭仁徵訪問稿〉，2020.6.11。

13　同前註。

有賽犬到我們基隆這邊來比賽，剛好在我辦公室窗戶外面，我就把這情境畫出來。我喜歡這個筆的線條。…它有一種快速跑步的感覺。[14]

此作中，可以看到蕭仁徵從具象轉向抽象的線條表現。如我在訪談中所言，「這感覺有點像遠山，可是近看它又像在奔跑的公鹿」；[15] 此部份以快速的筆觸，率性地勾勒而成、介於具象與抽象之間的遠景，使得整幅作品的構圖予人細膩且與眾不同的調性。

四、筆墨的自由度

此種直覺式的創作態度，也可見於蕭仁徵以自由的筆墨，詮釋出自己對傳統名作的再創造。如《早春》、《秋水長流》、《華山千仞》、《華山登頂》、《赤壁賦圖》等作，即是他以自由的筆墨轉譯傳統名作的皴法；而《秋水篇》則是他以繪畫的形式，對莊子名著的回應。

1977 年的《早春》一作，其靈感明顯地來自北宋畫家郭熙 1072 年的《早春圖》。郭熙的《早春圖》以充滿對於人物、屋舍、樹木、岩石、瀑布、河流、小徑等的細節描繪，以具象的圖繪，呈現出他在畫論〈林泉高致〉中，提到的「見青巒白道而思行，見平川落照而思望，見幽人山客而思居，見嚴扃泉石而思遊」[16] 之可行、可望、可居、可遊的山水空間；並以抖動圓轉的「雲頭皴」，表現出冬末春初時節，萬物復甦，一片欣欣向榮的景致。

不同於郭熙《早春圖》以具體且細微的描繪，勾勒出早春的氛圍；蕭仁徵的《早春》，選擇以抽象且粗獷的手法，再現出郭熙《早春圖》的意象。例如，蕭仁徵畫中三處主要的墨塊，即是狀寫郭熙《早春圖》中的主山與兩側的岩石。再者，蕭仁徵以飛白的圓形及向左上揚的筆觸，轉譯了郭熙《早春圖》中的「雲頭皴」及橫亘在山間的雲霧。最後，早春時節發出嫩芽的植物，及其即將爆發的生命力，蕭仁徵則選擇以黃色與鮮綠色表現之。簡言之，蕭仁徵的《早春》乃是以一種對待筆墨的自由態度，重現郭熙《早春圖》的氛圍。

蕭仁徵 1996 年的《秋水長流》，畫中的主角，乃是一道自高山上筆直而下的細長瀑布。如此的構圖，令人想起明代畫家沈周，為其師陳寬祝壽所繪的《廬山高》一作。沈周的《廬山高》，以十分緊密細膩的手法，刻劃出山體及岩石的走勢與肌理，就連瀑布後方的層山峻嶺，也毫不馬虎地細寫其獨特的形體與面貌。此外，筆直而下的長瀑，亦可見其源頭來自後方的山體之中。再者，沈周此作的筆法，也可見到繼承自元代畫家王蒙「解索皴」的運用。至於沈周《廬山高》所描繪的季節，也可從畫中依稀可見的楓葉得知，此時為秋天。

相較之下，蕭仁徵的《秋水長流》以一大片直率的紅色，及自群山峻嶺渲泄而下的瀑布，明指此作「秋水長流」的畫意。然而，與沈周《廬山高》一樣，蕭仁徵也清楚地交待瀑布的源頭始自後方的山體。值得注意的是，此作對於山石輪廓的描繪，亦顯得較為重視，且可同時見到粗、細、乾、濕、沉、滯、輕、快的筆墨運用。此種對於筆墨的自由度，頗似石濤《為禹老道兄作山水冊》一作中，提及「是法非法即成我法」的返璞歸真。

蕭仁徵 2003 年的《華山千仞》，描繪的是一座高聳直立的山體，以及周遭低矮圓緩的山石。以華山為題的畫作，較著名的有明代王履的《華山圖冊》，該圖冊中，除了可見王履對於華山各處奇景的精彩描繪之外，在崇山峻嶺以及烟嵐瀰漫之間，亦可見到旅人的身影。即使是近人

14　同前註。

15　同前註。

16　(宋) 郭熙、郭思父子撰，〈林泉高致〉，收入俞崑編著，《中國畫論類編》（臺北：華正書局，1984），頁 635。

張大千所繪的華山圖，也不乏遊覽其間的文人雅士。此種在山水畫中出現的點景人物，往往拉近觀者與繪畫的距離，彷彿觀畫者即是畫中的旅人，一起參與了遊覽山水的奇境之旅。

相較之下，蕭仁徵的《華山千仞》並非是要再現此種同遊的景象；反而更像是，畫家自己對華山獨特地質的探索。因此，該作中，我們可以看到畫家以類似墨拓的技法，以及如同毫芒的細線，表現山體的肌理；再以各種形狀的墨點與粗線，勾勒出山石的面目。而紙張略顯皺折的表面，也暗示千仞山石的粗糙質感。

蕭仁徵於 1998 年所繪的《秋水篇》，可謂是以分割畫面的形式，回應了《莊子‧秋水》中河神與海神的對話。《莊子‧秋水》以河神（河伯）與海神（北海若）的六段對話，展開一場對於人間世事及萬物價值判斷的探索與思辯。其形式，主要以河神提問，海神回答的方式進行之。我認為，蕭仁徵的《秋水篇》，或可將其視為以圖像反映了《莊子‧秋水》中，河神與海神的第五段對話。

首先，《秋水篇》上方的畫面，以濃得化不開的積墨、相互交疊的淡青色、淡赭色、灰色，以及時而交錯的飛白筆觸，呈現出莊子文中河伯的困惑與提問：「然則我何爲乎？何不爲乎？吾辭受趣捨，吾終奈何？」至於蕭仁徵此作下方的畫面，似呈現出北海若的回答：「道無終始，物有死生，不恃其成：一虛一滿，不位乎其形。……物之生也，若驟若馳，無動而不變，無時而不移。何爲乎？何不爲乎？夫固將自化。」換句話說，相較於蕭仁徵《秋水篇》上圖以筆墨的凝結與沉滯，暗示出河神的困惑與提問；那麼此作下圖流暢舒朗的筆墨表現，則意指海神對河神「萬物無定形而終將自然地變化」的解惑。

《赤壁賦圖》是蕭仁徵在 88 歲時，對傳統經典回應的書畫作品。此作以簡筆勾勒出一文士獨自划著小舟，面向一片以粗筆淡墨勾勒而成的山脈。其實，《赤壁賦圖》大量出現在南北宋之交，不論是宋代畫家楊士賢或者是金朝畫家武元直，其以蘇東坡《前赤壁賦》為底本所繪的《赤壁賦圖》，皆可見到直立千仞的連續山體，與江河中載有東坡、友人與船夫的小舟。然而，蕭仁徵《赤壁賦圖》的舟中，僅繪有一人，並有題記：「歲次二零一四年。甲午元日。於台灣七堵向陽草堂。關中投筆抗日志士。蕭仁徵書。時年八十有八。」從「甲午」（甲午戰爭）、「投筆抗日志士」（自我定位）、「台灣」（居住地）、「關中」（出生地）的線索或可推測，年輕時從中國大陸來到台灣的蕭仁徵，在面對臺灣近代史的「政治現實」之際，選擇以歷史情境相仿的南宋流行題材《赤壁賦圖》，並以自由率直的筆墨，安頓其近一甲子的創作思緒。

小結

最後，我想以 1961 年沈從文在〈抽象的抒情〉中所言「惟轉化爲文字，爲形象，爲音符，爲節奏，可望將生命某一種形式，某一種狀態，凝固下來」這一段話，作為蕭仁徵創作觀的結語。的確，不論是文學或繪畫，皆是人類欲以藝術美的形式，為這個「有情」的世界，留下自己曾經駐足過的吉光片羽。[17] 蕭仁徵的畫作，亦在大時代的洪流中，讓我們瞥見他以「質樸之心」所闡釋的有情世界。

17　王德威，〈「有情」的歷史—抒情傳統與中國文學現代性〉，《中國文哲研究集刊》第 33 期（2008.9），頁 80。

瓶花

Vase Flower

複合媒材　Mixed media　68.8×45.3cm　1995

風景中的詩意
Poetic Expression in Landscape Painting

臺灣畫壇於 1950 年代興起以現代抽象繪畫的純粹性，結合中國文藝抒情傳統，推敲琢磨人類精神性的風潮。投入現代抽象與抒情傳統的藝術創造生涯。

自學繪畫的蕭仁徵，創作自個人生活經驗出發。有別於學院派畫家，在此水墨現代化的浪潮中，提供我們思考藝術創作中的抒情傳統時，一個更直接且樸實的視角。

The 1950s in Taiwan saw a trend among art circles to combine the purity of modern abstract painting with Chinese literary and lyrical traditions as a way of speculating about human spirituality. Thus began the modern abstract and lyrical tradition.

Hsiao Jen-cheng taught himself painting during this period of rapid change in the art world. Unlike those with academic training, Hsiao draws from his own personal experiences, providing a more direct and humble angle of entry into the lyrical tradition.

一個世界

One World

彩墨 Ink and color 38.5×26.5cm 1956

雨中樹

Tree in the Rain

水彩　Watercolor　38.8×54cm　1958
國立臺灣美術館典藏　本次未展出

哀鳴

Wail

彩墨 Ink and color 54.5×39.4cm 1961

昇

Rise

水墨 Ink wash 26.5×38.8cm 1963
國立臺灣美術館典藏　本次未展出

山醉人醉

Mountain and Man,
Intoxicated

水彩 Watercolor
49×67.5cm 1969
臺北市立美術館典藏
本次未展出

水墨山水

Landscape in Ink Wash

水墨 Ink wash
38×53cm 1972
國立歷史博物館典藏
本次未展出

落日

Setting Sun

水墨 Ink wash 60×59.5cm 1973
國立歷史博物館典藏 本次未展出

寫意山水

Landscape in Expressive Brushstrokes

水墨 Ink wash 47×72.5cm 1973
國立歷史博物館典藏 本次未展出

沉醉

Intoxication

水彩 Watercolor 32×41cm 1979

馬祖酒廠

Matsu Liquor Factory

水彩 Watercolor 26.4×39cm 1993

基隆河上游

Source of the Keelung River

水彩 Watercolor 30.2×39.6cm

冬日

A Winter Day

複合媒材 Mixed media 54.5×39cm 1993

山水魂

Soul of Mountain and River

水墨 Ink wash 177.4×290.4cm 1993
國立臺灣美術館典藏 本次未展出

Ink Movement
Hsiao Jen-cheng and the Expansion of Modern Painting

天山泉聲

Water Spring on Celestial Mountain

複合媒材　Mixed media　158×98×2C cm　1995
雙聯屏

Ink Movement
Hsiao Jen-cheng and the Expansion of Modern Painting

濱海之晨

Morning on the Seaside

水彩 Watercolor
37×53cm 1995

太陽浪濤

Sun and Wave

複合媒材　Mixed media　239×59.5×3C cm　1995
三聯屏

春之舞

Dance in Spring

複合媒材 Mixed media 180×180cm 1998

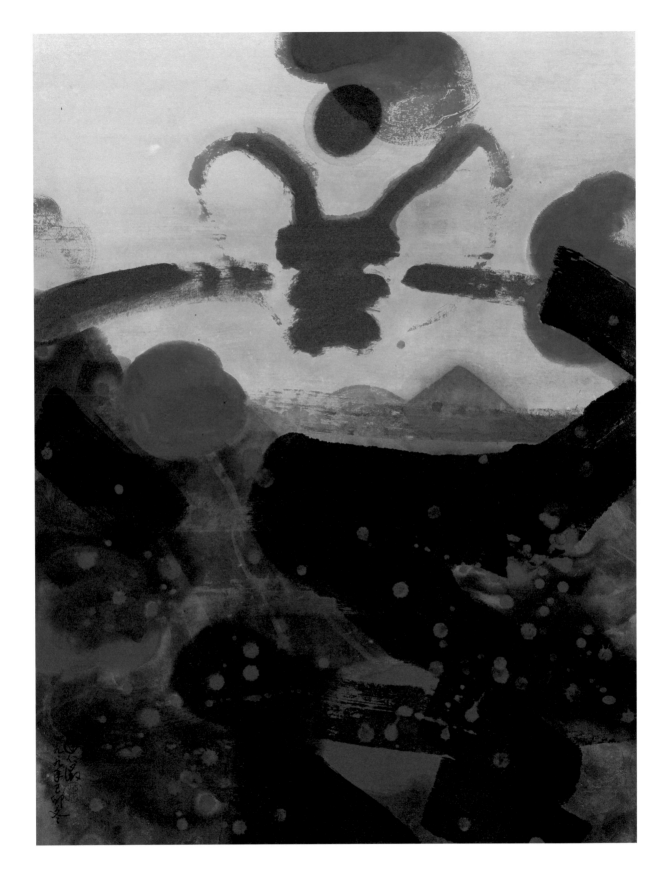

龍瑞雲祥

Auspicious Dragon and Clouds

複合媒材 Mixed media 88×68cm 1999

追日

In Pursuit of Sun

彩墨 Ink and color 39×27cm 2000

玉山高

Elevated Jade Mountain

複合媒材　Mixed media　180×186cm　2002
雙聯屏

虎山行

Off to the Tiger Mountain

複合媒材 Mixed media
138×35cm 2009

紅峰

Red Ridges

複合媒材　Mixed media
135.5×35cm　2009

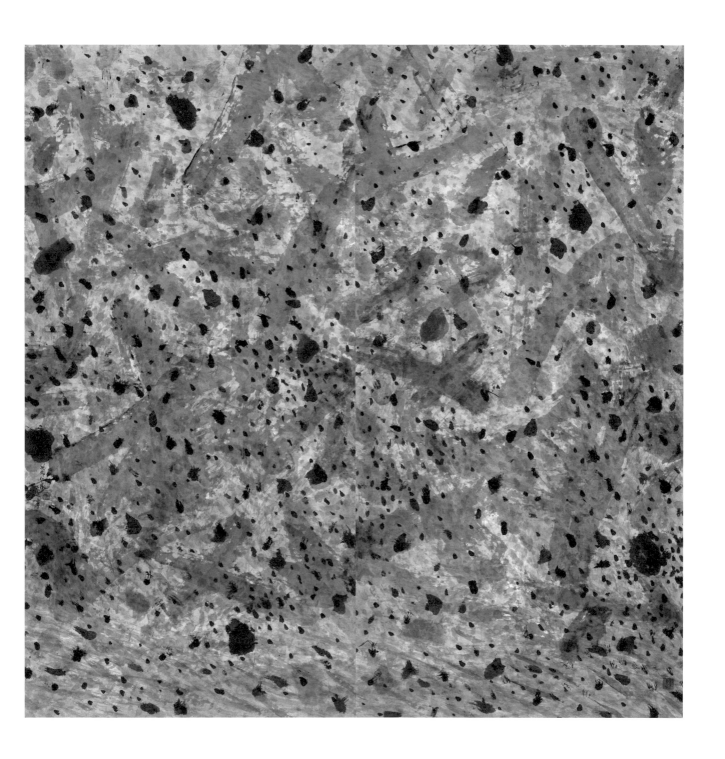

江水東流

River Flowing East

複合媒材　Mixed media　136×69.5×2C cm　2013
雙聯屏

墨韻

蕭仁徵 現代畫開拓展

52

華嶽登頂

Climbing on the Top of the
Mount Hua

複合媒材 Mixed media
223×52.5×6C cm 2015

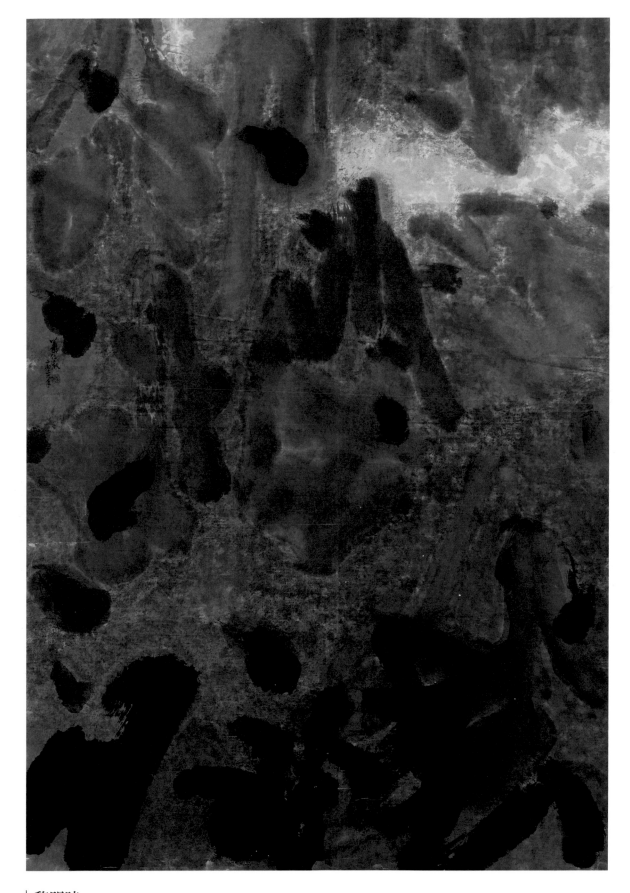

黎明時

Dawn

複合媒材 Mixed media 155×110cm 2016

紅崖

Red Ridges

彩墨 Ink and color 67.8×69.5cm 2016

雲山相依

Clouds Leaning on Mountain

彩墨 Ink and color 137.5×67.5×2C cm 2019
雙聯屏

玉山青

Green Jade Mountain

複合媒材　Mixed media
240×124cm　2021

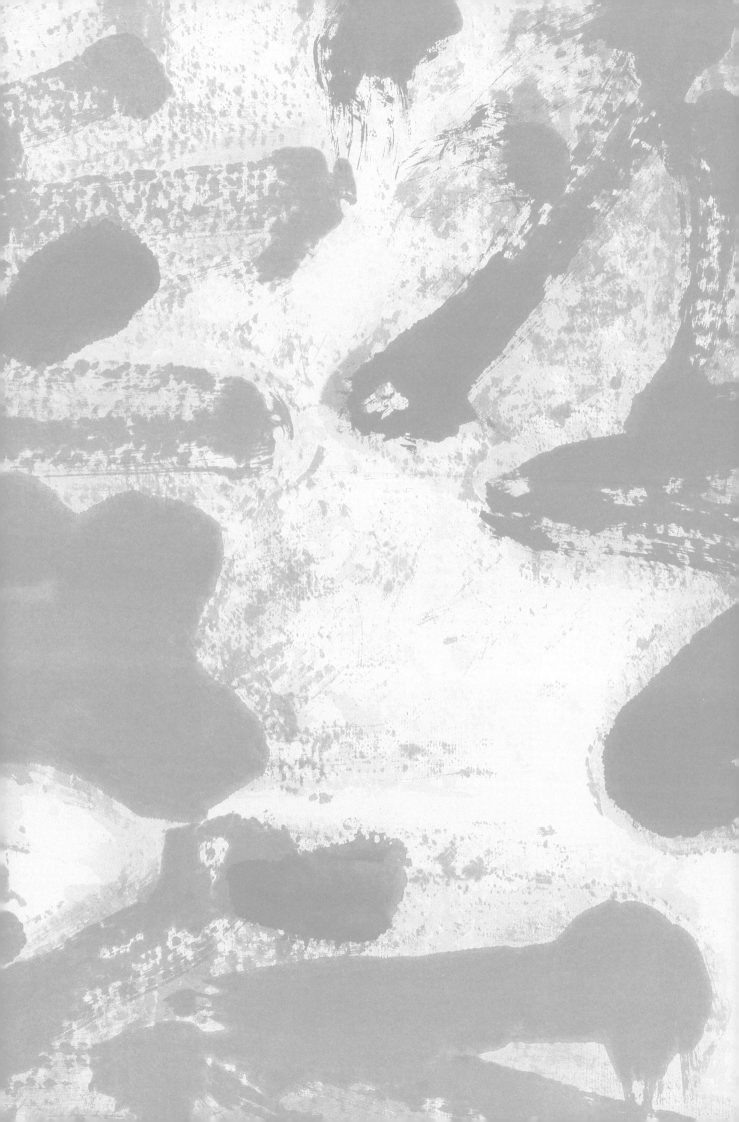

直覺性的創造
Intuitive Art

蕭氏的創作奠基於其直覺式的美感經驗，不受學院技巧與師承束縛，以實驗性的複合媒材藝術表現，進行詩意的畫面結構探索。此在創作過程中的探索，逐漸鋪展為蕭氏對視覺之美的追求。

此系列創作標誌著藝術家自具象摹寫轉向抽象詩意的線條表現，快速的筆觸、率性地勾勒，凝聚為介於具象與抽象之間的風景，終於構成蕭氏作品與眾不同的調性。

Hsiao's work is based on his own intuitive aesthetic sense, not bound by academic technique or teachings. By experimenting with different forms of media, Hsiao explores the poetic resonance of different compositions, gradually building his personal sense of visual beauty.

This set of highly abstract work marks the artist's transition from strict representation to linear abstraction and poeticism. Rapid brushstrokes freely trace landscape views, intertwining the material and the abstract to form the distinctive tone that defines Hsiao's work.

阿珠

A-chu

彩墨 Ink and color 27×19.5cm 1958

人體

Human Body

水彩 Watercolor 38.5×26.5cm 1963

黑美人

Black Beauty

彩墨　Ink and color　38×26.5cm　2004

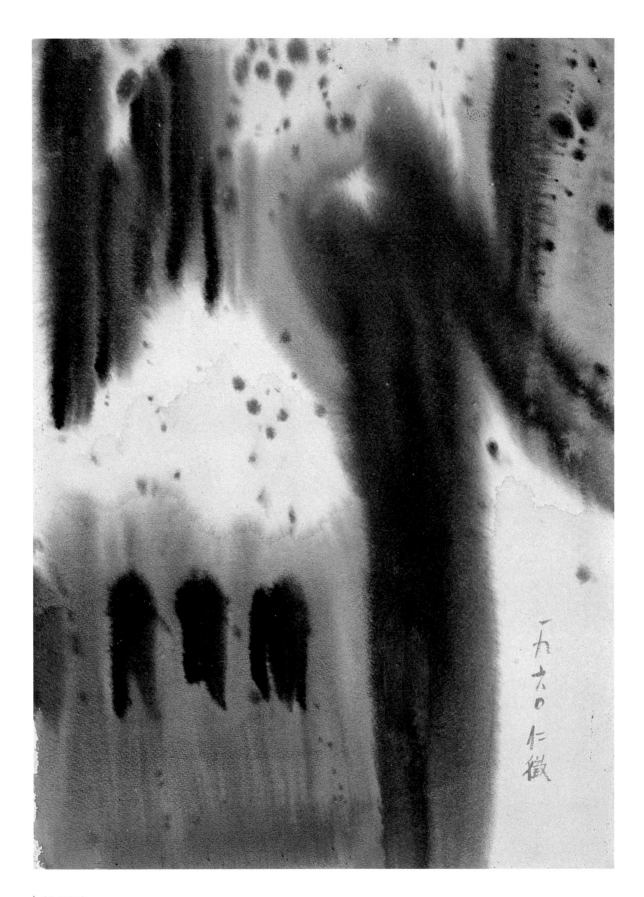

離別時

Departure

水彩 Watercolor 52×38.5cm 1960
臺北市立美術館典藏　本次未展出

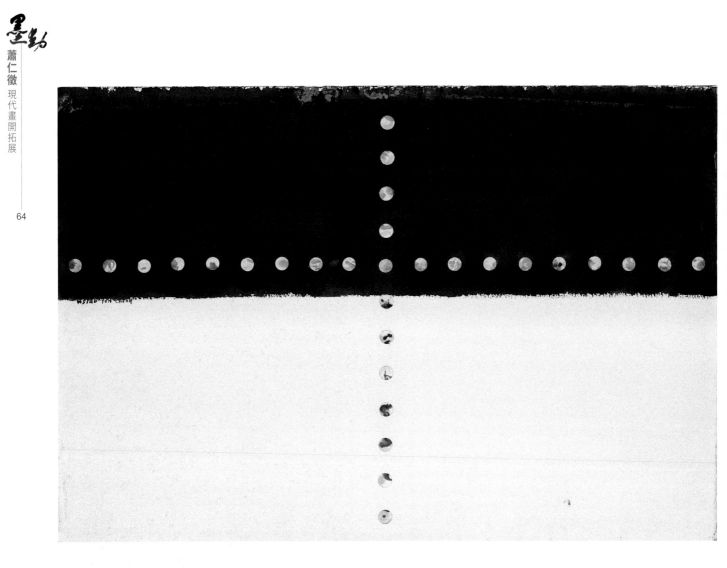

星光燦爛

Splendid Stars

版畫 Print 38×53cm 1968
國立歷史博物館典藏　本次未展出

盛世

Zenith of the Time

彩墨 Ink and color
135×69cm 1982

浴火鳳凰

Phoenix

複合媒材　Mixed media　54.5×39cm　2000

無題 4

Untitled, No. 4

複合媒材　Mixed media
137.5×23cm　2002

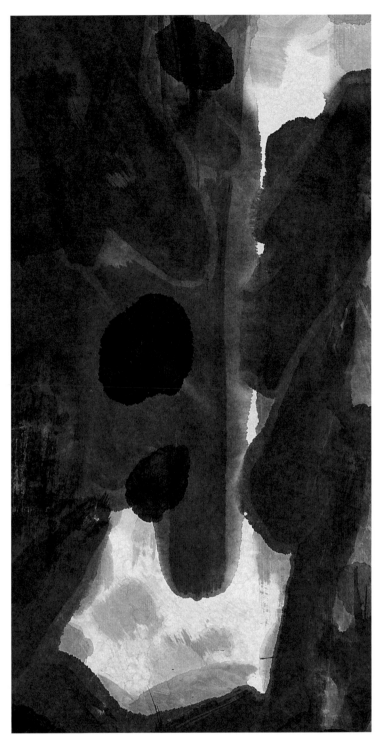

無題 6

Untitled, No. 6

複合媒材　Mixed media
137.5×23.5cm　2002

無題 15

Untitled, No. 15

複合媒材 Mixed media
137.5×26cm 2002

無題 5

Untitled, No. 5

複合媒材　Mixed media
137.5×23cm　2003

無題 16

Untitled, No. 16

複合媒材 Mixed media
138×35cm 2004

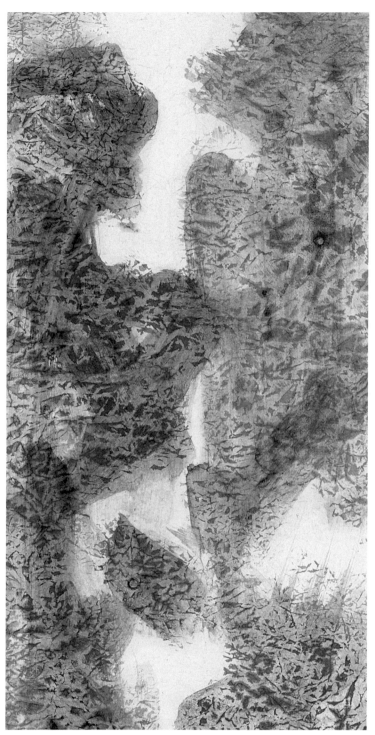

無題 9

Untitled, No. 9

複合媒材 Mixed media
137.5×23.5cm 2005

無題 10

Untitled, No. 10

複合媒材 Mixed media
137.5×23.5cm 2005

無題 11

Untitled, No. 11

複合媒材　Mixed media
137.5×23.5cm　2005

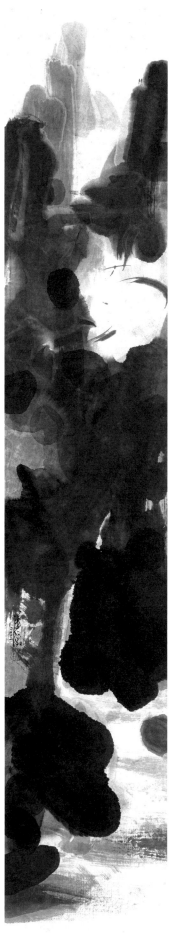

無題 13

Untitled, No. 13

複合媒材 Mixed media
137.5×23.5cm 2005

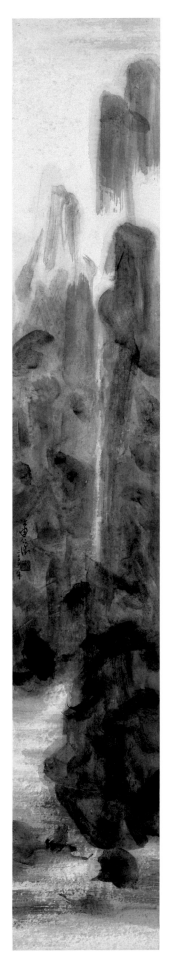

無題 14

Untitled, No. 14

複合媒材 Mixed media
137.5×23.5cm 2005

無題 2

Untitled, No. 2

複合媒材 Mixed media
137.5×23.5cm 2006

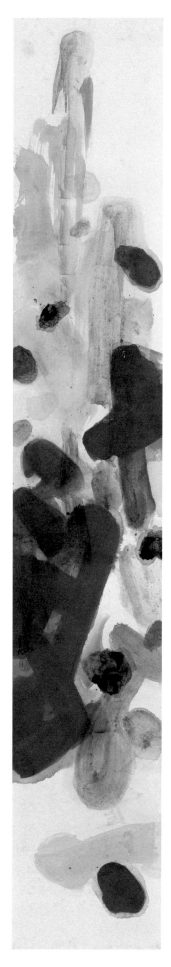

無題 3

Untitled, No. 3

複合媒材　Mixed media
137.5×23.5cm　2006

無題 7

Untitled, No. 7

複合媒材　Mixed media
137.5×23.5cm　2006

Ink Movement
Hsiao Jen-cheng and the Expansion of Modern Painting

無題 8

Untitled, No. 8

複合媒材 Mixed media
137.5×23.5cm 2007

無題 12

Untitled, No. 12

複合媒材 Mixed media
137.5×23.5cm 2007

無題 17

Untitled, No. 17

複合媒材　Mixed media
137.5×35cm　2007

無題 1

Untitled, No. 1

複合媒材 Mixed media
179×32cm 2009

蕭仁徵 現代畫開拓展

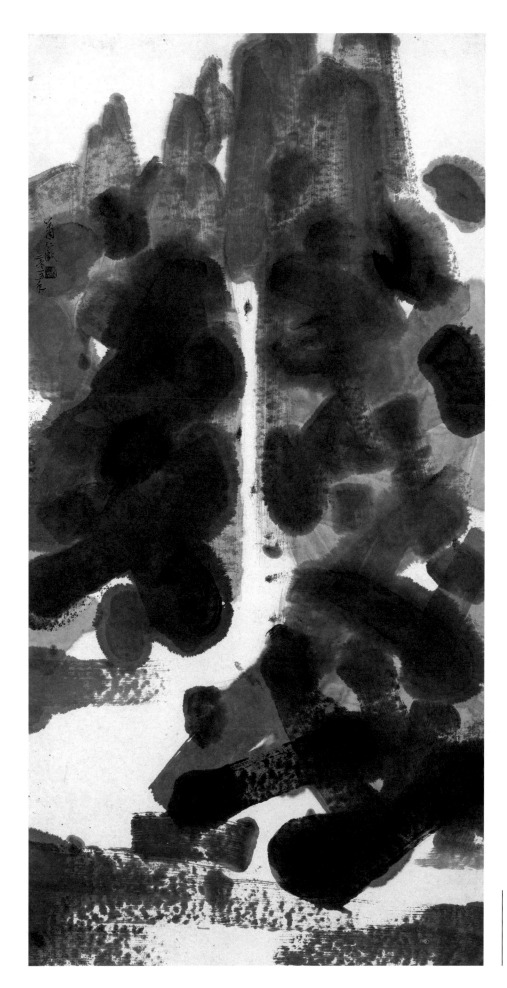

無題 13

Untitled, No. 13

複合媒材 Mixed media
135×69cm 2015

無題 11

Untitled, No. 11

複合媒材　Mixed media
181×96cm　2017

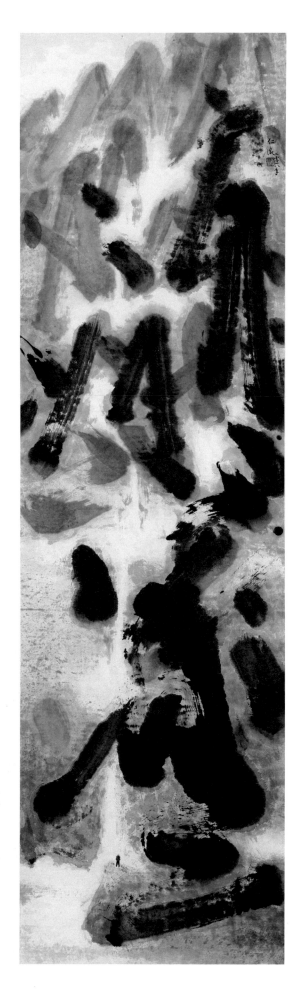

無題 No. 2

Untitled, No. 2

複合媒材　Mixed media
185×95cm　2018

無題 No. 14

Untitled, No. 14

複合媒材 Mixed media
135×69cm 2018

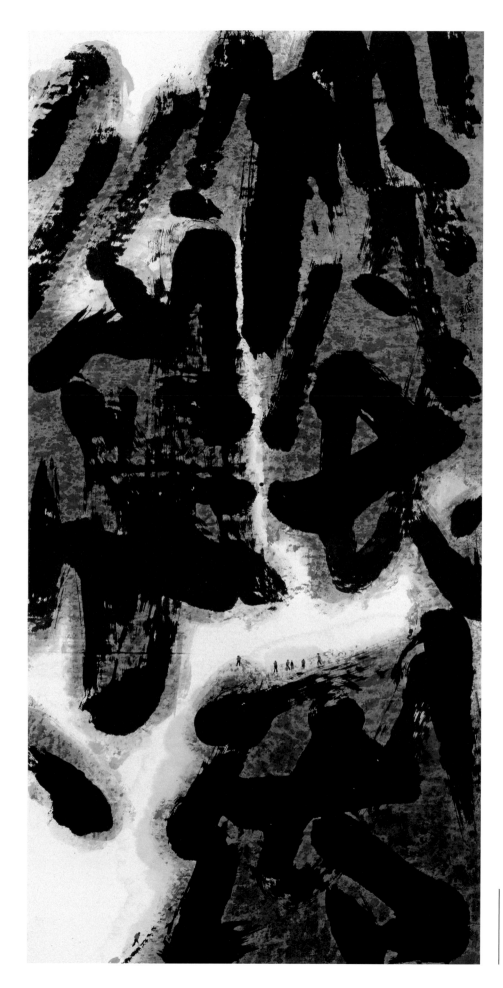

無題 No. 18

Untitled, No. 18

複合媒材　Mixed media
135×68cm　2018

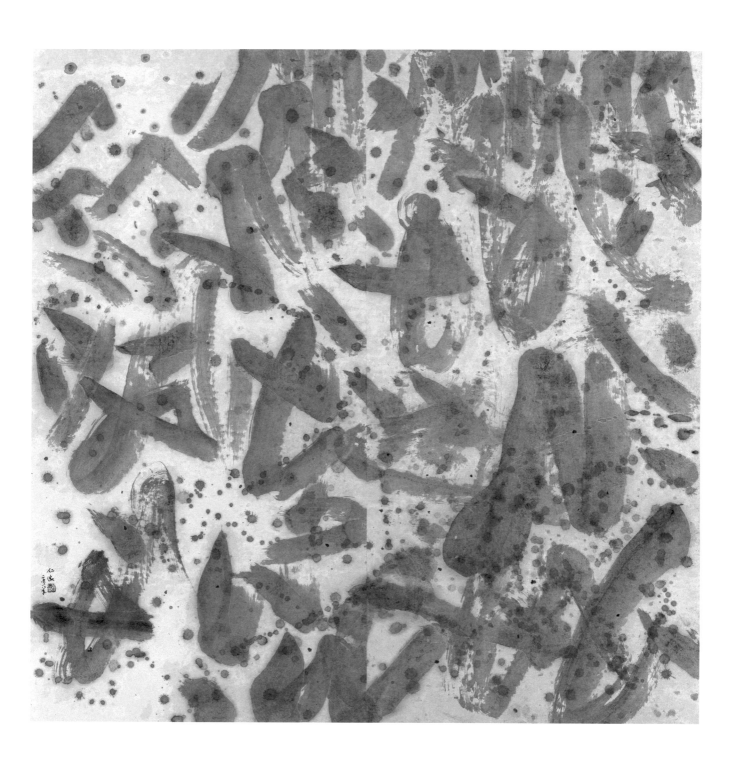

無題 No. 23

Untitled, No. 23

複合媒材　Mixed media
135×135cm　2018

無題 No. 24

Untitled, No. 24

複合媒材 Mixed media
135×67cm 2019

無題 No. 15

Untitled, No. 15

複合媒材 Mixed media
135×69cm 2019

無題 No. 3

Untitled, No. 3

複合媒材　Mixed media　179×96cm　2019

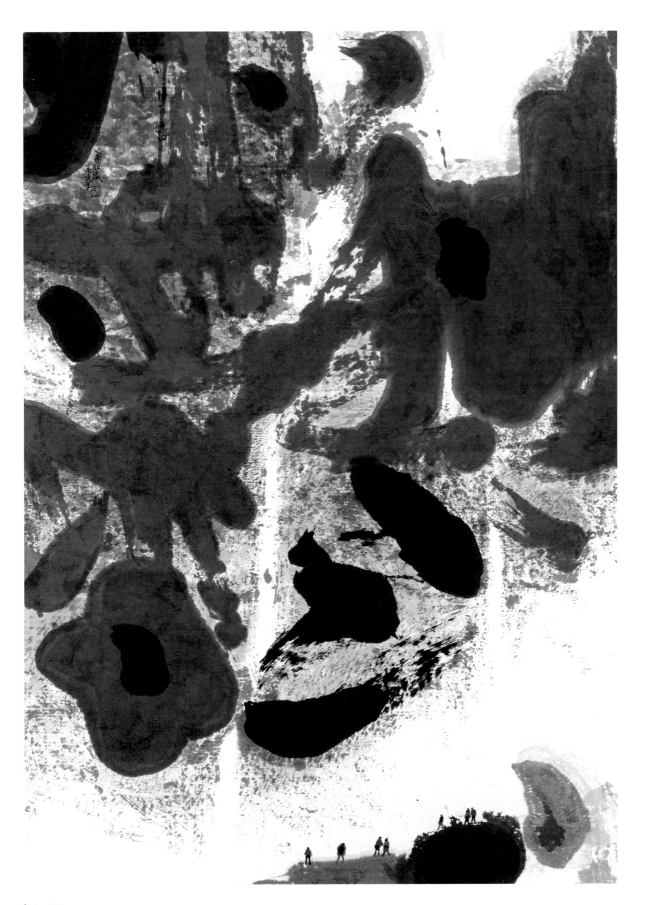

無題 No. 4

Untitled, No. 4

複合媒材 Mixed media 134×96cm 2019

無題 No. 5

Untitled, No. 5

複合媒材　Mixed media　165×83cm　2019

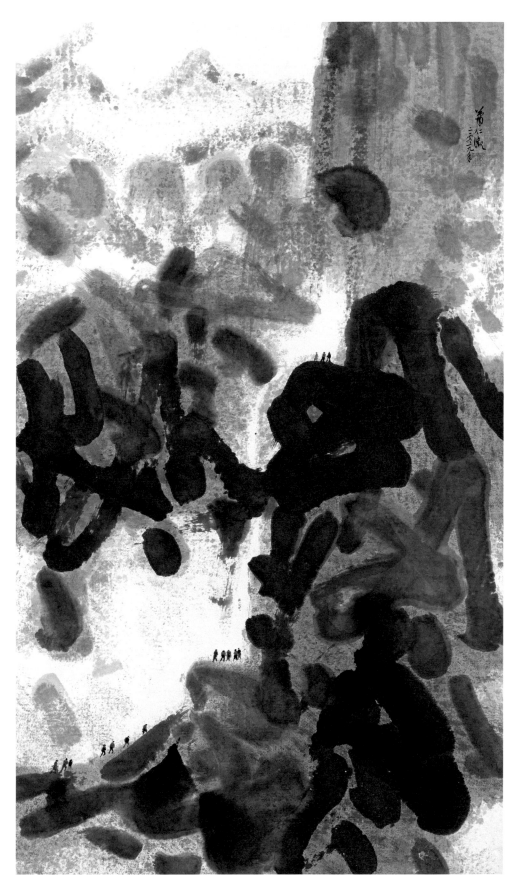

無題 No. 6

Untitled, No. 6

複合媒材 Mixed media 163×96cm 2019

無題 No. 7

Untitled, No. 7

複合媒材 Mixed media 167×95cm 2019

無題 No. 8

Untitled, No. 8

複合媒材 Mixed media 158×91cm 2019

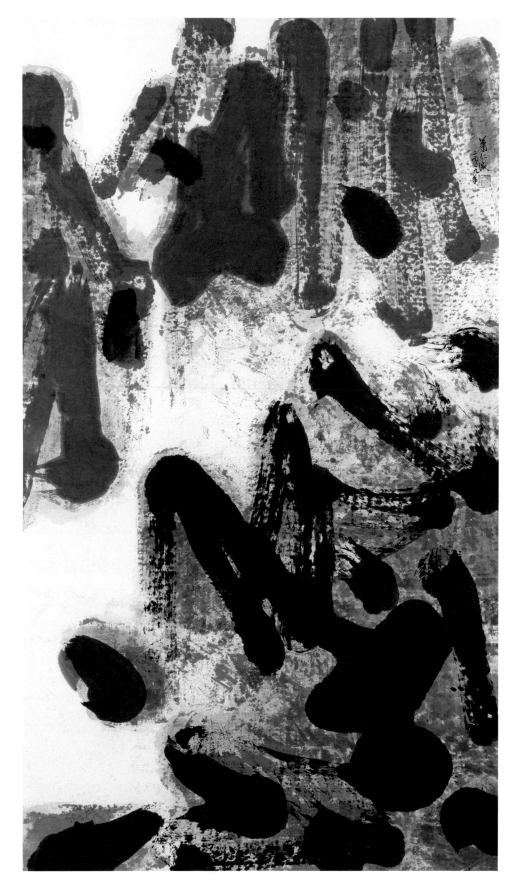

無題 No. 9

Untitled, No. 9

複合媒材 Mixed media 165×96cm 2019

無題 No. 10

Untitled, No. 10

複合媒材 Mixed media 179×97cm 2019

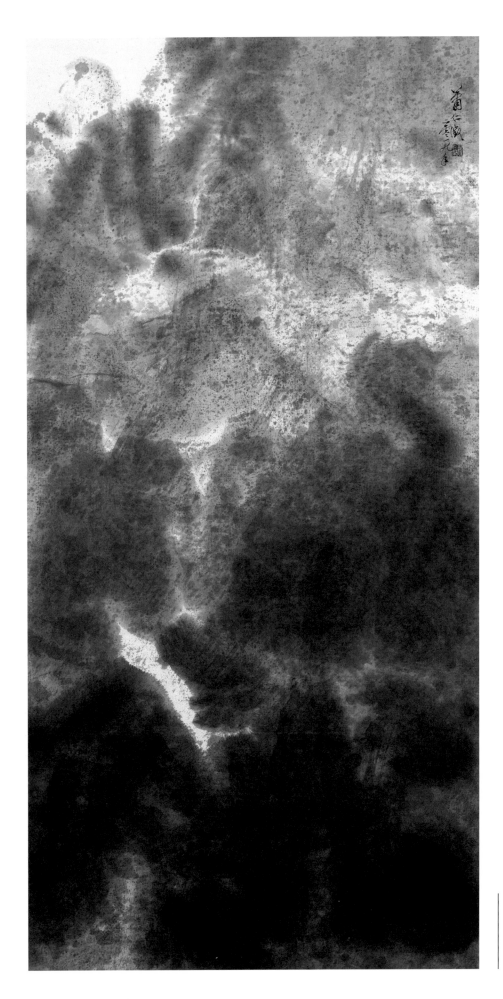

無題 No. 21

Untitled, No. 21

複合媒材 Mixed media
135×68cm 2019

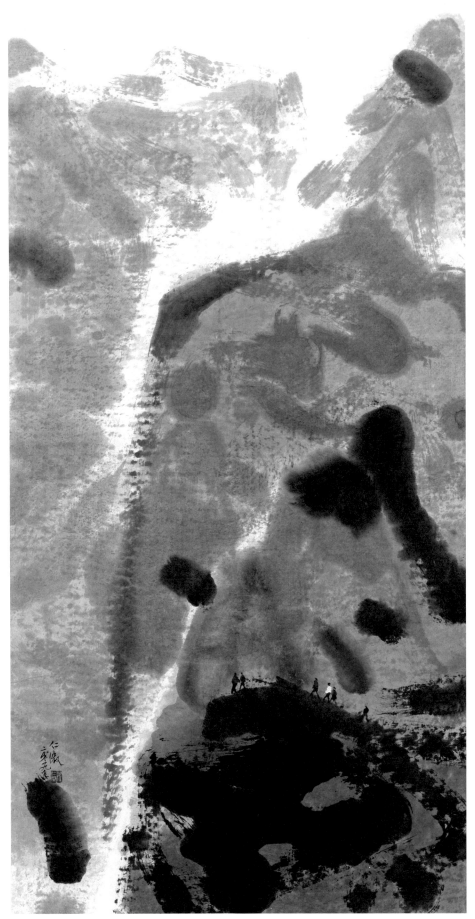

無題 No. 22

Untitled, No. 22

複合媒材 Mixed media
135×68cm 2019

No. 29 無題

Untitled, No. 29

複合媒材 Mixed media
136×69.5cm 2019

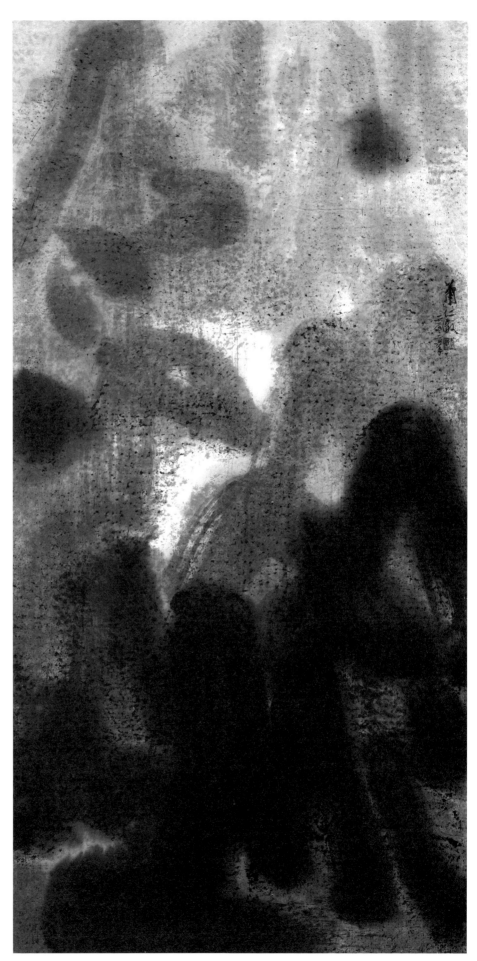

No. 28 無題

Untitled, No. 28

複合媒材 Mixed media
134.5×68.5cm 2020

無題 No. 12

Untitled, No. 12

複合媒材 Mixed media
135×69cm 2020

無題 No. 16

Untitled, No. 16

複合媒材 Mixed media
135×69cm 2020

無題 No. 19

Untitled, No. 19

複合媒材　Mixed media
135×68cm　2020

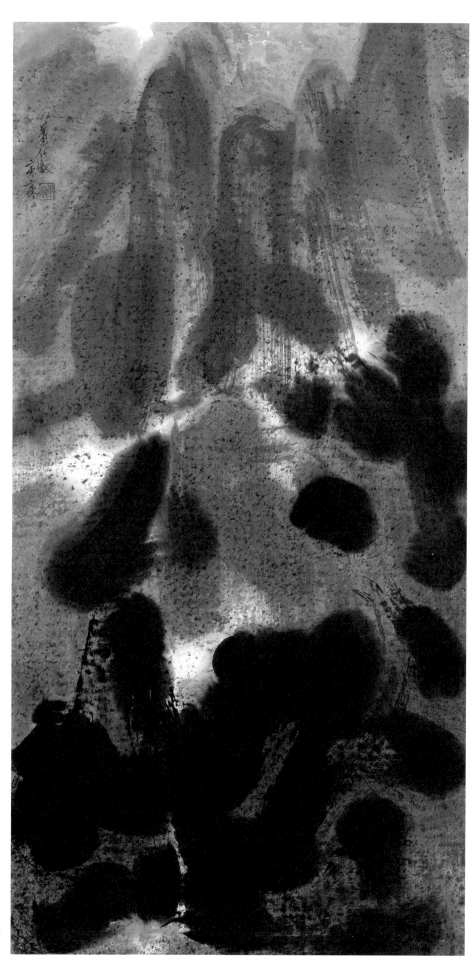

無題 No. 25

Untitled, No. 25

複合媒材 Mixed media
135×68cm 2020

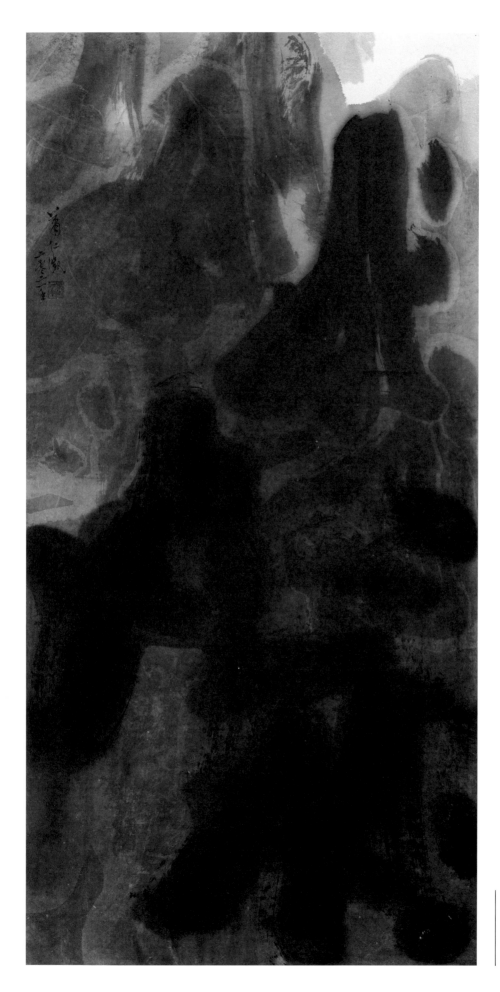

無題 No. 26

Untitled, No. 26

複合媒材 Mixed media
135×68cm 2021

13 點 15 分

13:15

複合媒材 Mixed media
177.5×59cm 2020

筆墨自由及其他
Liberation of Brushwork and Other Forms

蕭氏取材自書法、水墨傳統的創作，多以自由的筆墨轉譯傳統名作
法式嚴謹的布局皴擦，以繪畫形式回探人與景物相遇之初的感動。
清初大家石濤曾言：「筆墨當隨時代」、「是法非法即成我法」，
推崇繪畫表現中的返璞歸真。蕭氏於繪畫中自學不輟，藉書報展覽
之媒遍覽書畫名家精作，於創作時則自由率直地在大時代的洪流中，
以筆墨安頓其近一甲子的美感追求，讓我們瞥見他以「質樸之心」
所闡釋的有情世界。

Some of Hsiao's works are informed by traditional calligraphy and
ink painting. For these paintings, he often adopts freeform brushwork
to interpret classic compositions and textures of well-known works,
exploring the sensations felt when first encountering a landscape.

To promote a return to original expressionist principles of painting, Shi
Tao, a famous painter of the early Qing Dynasty, used to say, "Brushwork
should follow one's own time" and "Joining methods will be my
method." Hsiao taught himself to paint by reading and viewing great
works in newspapers, magazines, and exhibitions. When he paints, he
freely wields the brush in aesthetic pursuit of the turbulence of his era,
creating a sentient world as interpreted by his humility.

早春
Early Spring
彩墨 Ink and color 39×27.5cm 1977

長相思

Longing

水墨 Ink wash　83.5×69cm　1991

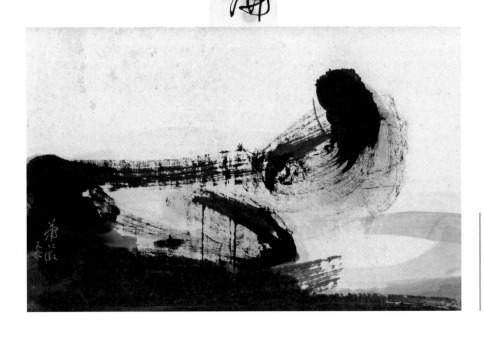

秋水篇

Chuang Tzu's "The Floods of Autumn"

彩墨 Ink and color
138×69cm 1998

秋水篇（上部）

山水冊頁集

Album of Landscape Paintings

冊頁 Album 46×46cm

(節錄，原作共 31 件)

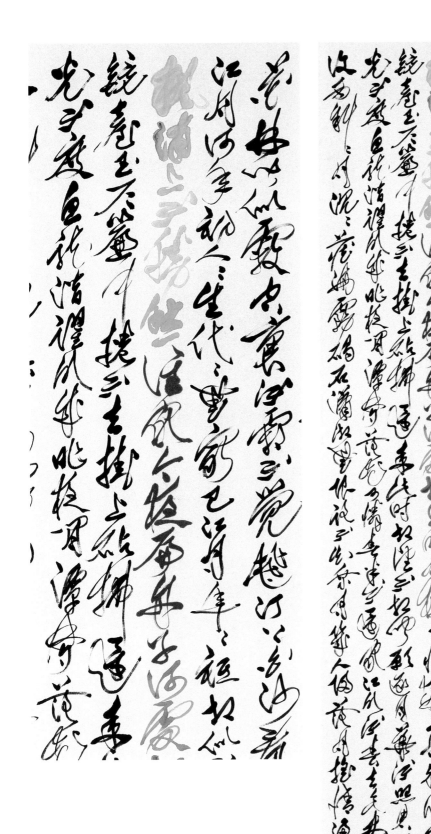

春江花月夜

Spring River and a Night of
Flower and Moon

彩墨 / 書法 Ink and color/ calligraphy
135.5×23.5cm 2012

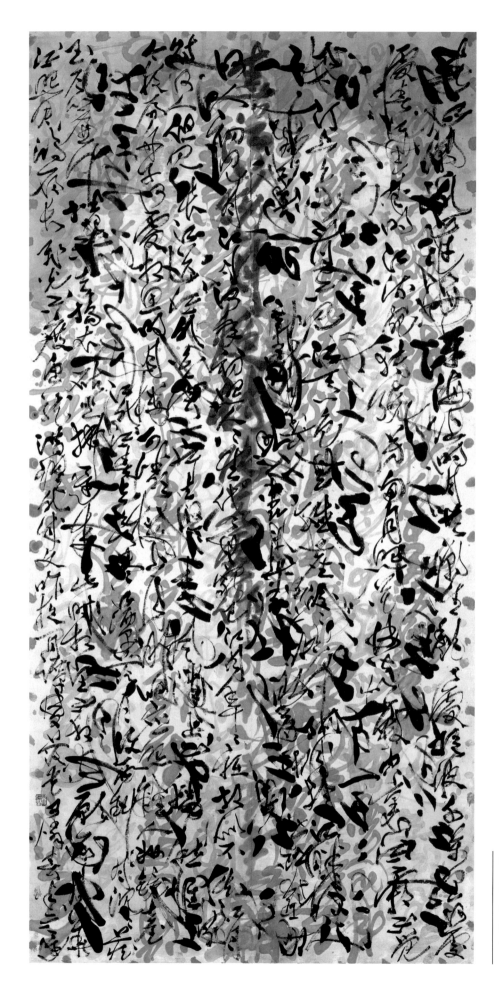

春江花月夜

Spring River and a Night
of Flower and Moon
彩墨 / 書法 Ink and color/
calligraphy
135×68.5cm 2016

蘇軾詞

Su Shi's Poems

彩墨 / 書法 Ink and color/ calligraphy
136×35cm

陶淵明桃花源

Peach Blossom Spring by Tao Yuan-ming

彩墨 / 書法　Ink and color/ calligraphy
136.5×23.5cm

李白詩

Li Bo's Poems

彩墨 / 書法 Ink and color/ calligraphy
135.5×23.5cm

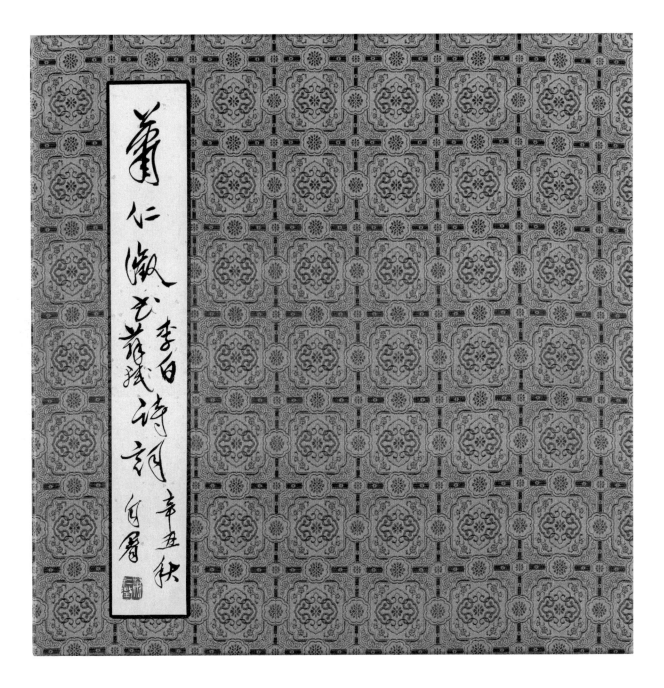

書法冊頁集

Album of Calligraphy

冊頁　Album　46×46cm

(節錄，原作共 26 篇)

印禪撰聯　見性明心

Couplet of "Seeing One's
Nature and Understanding
One's Mind," by Chan Pi-chin

書法 Calligraphy 160×32cm 2012
作者：詹碧琴（蕭仁徵先生夫人）

印禪詹阿仁詩

"Poem by Chan A-ren," by Chan Pi-chin

書法　Calligraphy　70×67.7cm　2014
作者：詹碧琴（蕭仁徵先生夫人）

蕭仁徵畫像

Portrait of Hsiao Jen-cheng in Drawing, by Chang Hsin-chuan

素描 35.5x25.5cm 1955
作者：張性荃

蕭仁徵畫像

Portrait of Hsiao Jen-cheng, by Max Liu

水彩 Watercolor 39.5x26cm 1968
作者：劉其偉

舞者（1）

Dancer, 1
素描 Sketch 39×26.6cm

墨韻
蕭仁徵 現代畫開拓展

舞者（2）

Dancer, 2

素描 Sketch 39×26.2cm

舞者（3）

Dancer, 3
素描 Sketch 39.5×34.5cm

附錄
Appendix

我回憶自己繪製作品的過程，這也不是說胸有成竹，或有
一個模樣，完全不是！只有一個想法，就是要表現某一種
畫的一個想法，或將一個人物的樣子畫出來，這是第一
個。第二個呢，就是我不知道要畫什麼，但是我畫筆一下
去，兩、三筆以後，我就知道我要畫什麼，這是我做抽象
畫的一個性格。

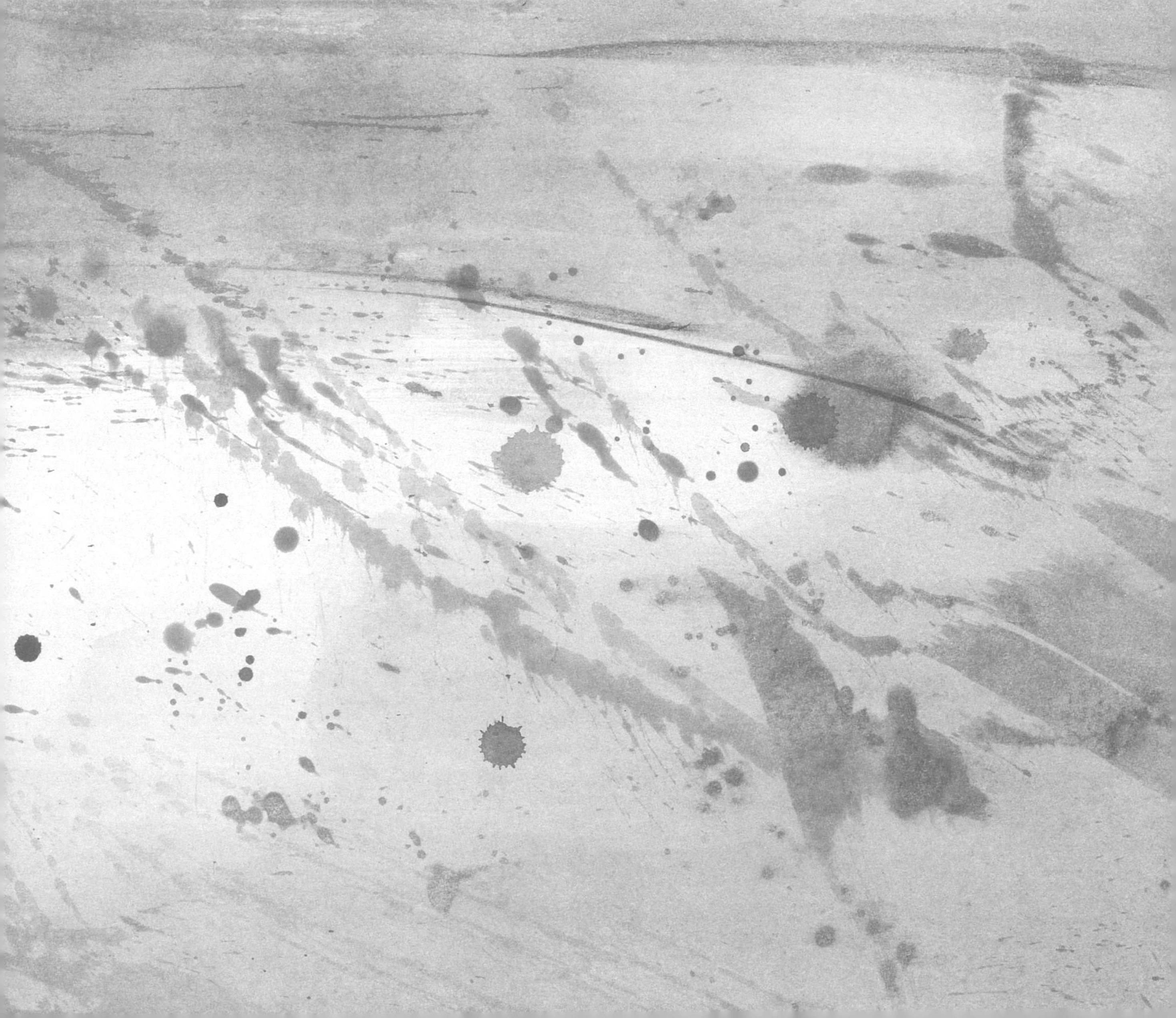

蕭仁徵創作年表
Chronology

1925 年（民國 14 年）

· 5 月 28 日出生於陝西省周至縣九峰鄉懷道村黃家堡（今陝西省西安市鄠邑區蔣村鎮懷道村黃家堡），父蕭伯正、母范氏。

1931 年（民國 20 年）

· 隨家母至同村員府，見壁上書畫依依不捨，回家試畫《梅花喜鵲圖》，爾後於就讀私塾時，常見員濟博先生作畫，深受其影響。

1935 年（民國 24 年）

· 就讀「祖庵鎮高級中心小學」，於圖畫課受鞏育勤先生教導，初立美術書畫之基礎。

1943 年（民國 32 年）

· 考入「私立武成初級中學」，於美術課以臨摹習畫。

1944 年（民國 33 年）

· 在校報名志願從軍，至雲南省曲靖市受嚴格軍事訓練，隔年對日抗戰勝利後，隨軍前往遼寧省。

1946 年（民國 35 年）

· 復學就讀「國防部預備幹部局特設長春青年中學」，於該校美術課學習中、西畫，假日則於長春市「文英畫社」學習素描，常於教室作畫至深夜不倦。

1947 年（民國 36 年）

· 轉讀「國防部預備幹部局特設嘉興青年中學」，於該校美術課學習中、西畫，並常去杭州市西湖等地寫生。

1949 年（民國 38 年）

· 隨軍來臺灣，假日常外出寫生。

1950 年（民國 39 年）

· 3 月參加「臺灣省國民學校專科（美術科）教員試驗」檢定合格。

· 以《秋菊圖》面試，於臺北市「飛馬畫社」擔任設計師。

1951 年（民國 40 年）

· 考取「中國美術協會」美術研究班，師事陳定山、朱德群、黃榮燦等學習中、西畫。

· 於臺北市「上海美藝廣告公司」擔任設計師。

1952 年（民國 41 年）

· 於臺北市「世界廣告工程公司」擔任設計師。

1953 年（民國 42 年）

‧陸續於多所國民小學、國民中學與「臺灣省立基隆市高級商工職業學校」、「臺灣省立花蓮師範專科學校」等任繪畫導師，並開始參加「臺灣省教員美術展覽會」。

1955 年（民國 44 年）

‧參加「自由中國畫展」，於臺北市「新聞大樓」展出。

‧參加「新綠水彩畫會」水彩畫展，於臺北市「中山堂」展出。

1956 年（民國 45 年）

‧參加「中國現代美展」，於「臺北市教育會」二樓展出。

1957 年（民國 46 年）

‧以水彩畫作品《南門風景》參加第四屆「中華民國全國美術展覽會」入選，於「國立臺灣藝術館」展出。

1959 年（民國 48 年）

‧成立「長風畫會」，與張熾昌、吳鼎藩等為共同發起人。

‧以半抽象水彩畫作品《雨中樹》入選「法國巴黎國際雙年藝展」，於法國巴黎展出。

‧以抽象水彩畫作品《森林之舞》入選第十四屆「臺灣省全省美術展覽會」，於「臺灣省立博物館」展出。

1960 年（民國 49 年）

‧第一屆「長風畫展」，於臺北市「新聞大樓」展出。

‧以抽象水墨畫作品《春》、《夏》兩幅入選「香港國際現代繪畫沙龍展」，於香港「聖約翰禮拜堂」副堂展出。

1961 年（民國 50 年）

‧第二屆「長風畫展」，於臺北市「新聞大樓」展出。

‧以抽象彩墨畫作品《災難》、《哀鳴》兩幅入選「巴西聖保羅國際雙年藝展」，於巴西聖保羅市展出。

1962 年（民國 51 年）

‧第三屆「長風畫展」，於「國立臺灣藝術館」展出。

‧舉行個人首次畫展「蕭仁徵水彩水墨個展」，於「基隆市議會」（前）禮堂展出。

‧受邀參加「國立歷史博物館」主辦「現代彩墨展」展出。

1963 年（民國 52 年）

・第四屆「長風畫展」，於臺北市「國際畫廊」展出。

・參加「臺灣省教員美術展覽會」，雕塑部作品《童顏》獲優選獎，於臺中市巡迴展出。

・受邀參加「國立歷史博物館」主辦「全國水彩畫展覽」展出。

1964 年（民國 53 年）

・成立「中國現代水墨畫會」，與于還素、劉國松等為共同發起人。

・受聘擔任「中國家庭教育協進會」繪畫部評審委員。

・加入「國際藝術教育協會」（INSEA）。

・應「國立臺灣藝術館」邀請，參加「中國現代水墨畫展覽」。

・參加「中國聯合水彩畫展」，於臺北市「新聞大樓」展出。

・應日本「きのくにや畫廊」邀請，參加「臺灣水彩畫家作品展覽」，於東京展出。

・參加「臺灣省教員美術展覽會」西畫部，水彩畫作品《海邊》、《雨後情》入選展出。

1965 年（民國 54 年）

・考入「國立臺灣藝術專科學校」美術科。

・應「國立歷史博物館」邀請，參加「日華美術交誼展覽」，於東京「上野公園」展出。

1966 年（民國 55 年）

・獲「國際藝術教育協會」（INSEA）提名為亞洲區候選委員。

1968 年（民國 57 年）

・成立「中國水墨畫學會」，與劉國松等為共同發起人。

1969 年（民國 58 年）

・「國立臺灣藝術專科學校」美術科畢業。

・參加「中國現代水墨畫會」展覽，於臺北市「耕莘文教院」展出。

・應「國立歷史博物館」邀請，參加西班牙「國立現代藝術館」之「中國現代藝術展覽」、
歐洲八國之「中華民國文物歐洲巡迴展覽」巡迴展出。

・應「國立歷史博物館」邀請，參加「中國藝術特展」於紐西蘭、澳大利亞、斐濟等國計
二十餘城市巡迴展出。

1970 年（民國 59 年）

・臺北市「凌雲畫廊」舉辦馬白水、洪瑞麟、劉其偉、王藍、張杰、蕭仁徵、席德進、高山
嵐八位名家水彩畫聯展，抽象水墨畫作品《構成》為巴西駐華大使繆勒典藏。

・參加「中國現代水墨畫展」，於臺北市「國立臺灣藝術館」展出。

・應「臺灣省立博物館」邀請，舉行「蕭仁徵水彩、彩墨個人畫展」。

1971 年（民國 60 年）

· 受聘擔任「國立歷史博物館」主辦「亞洲兒童畫展」評審委員。
· 應「國立歷史博物館」邀請，參加「當代畫家近作展」展出。
· 應「國立歷史博物館」邀請，參加「日華現代美術展覽」，於東京「上野公園」展出。
· 參加「中國水墨畫大展」，於「臺灣省立博物館」展出。

1972 年（民國 61 年）

· 參加「中國水墨畫大展」，於「香港大會堂」展出。

· 1973 年（民國 62 年）

· 應「國立歷史博物館」邀請，參加「中國現代水墨畫展」展出。
· 應「黎明文化中心」邀請，參加「名家作品聯展」展出。
· 參加「全國水彩畫大展」，於「臺灣省立博物館」展出。

1974 年（民國 63 年）

· 應「國立國父紀念館」邀請，參加「當代畫家近作展」展出。

1975 年（民國 64 年）

· 應「國立國父紀念館」邀請，參加「全國水彩畫名家作品特展」展出。
· 應「中國文藝協會」邀請，參加「水彩畫名家展」展出，作品《構成》為女作家張蘭熙典藏。

1976 年（民國 65 年）

· 應英國「LYL 美術館」邀請，參加「中國當代十人水墨畫特展」展出，山水畫兩幅為該館典藏。
· 應「基隆市立圖書館」邀請，舉行個人畫展於該館「文藝活動中心」。

1977 年（民國 66 年）

· 成立「基隆市美術協會」，為該協會之發起人。
· 應「基隆市立圖書館」邀請，參加「中國現代名家作品聯展」展出。

1978 年（民國 67 年）

· 於「基隆市美術協會」擔任常務理事。
· 應臺北市「春之藝廊」邀請，參加「現代水墨畫聯展」展出。
· 受聘擔任中華民國第九屆「世界兒童畫展」評審委員。

1979 年（民國 68 年）

· 「藝術家畫廊」舉行「蕭仁徵現代水墨、水彩畫個展」，作品《龍與雲》、《良駒》、《寒冬》為東京「大通銀行」典藏。
· 應「美國在臺協會」邀請，於「美國在臺協會文化中心」舉行個人畫展。

1980 年（民國 69 年）

· 「藝術家畫廊」舉行「蕭仁徵現代水墨畫個展」，作品《太陽》、《冬日》、《長相思》、《海景》為美國「大通銀行」及德國收藏家典藏。

1981 年（民國 70 年）

· 應「中國電視公司」邀請，參加「水墨畫家作品展」展出。

1982 年（民國 71 年）

· 應「基隆市政府」函聘，擔任「全國美術創作展覽」籌備委員暨評審委員。

· 應「行政院文化建設委員會」函邀，推薦為「文藝季縣市地方美展計畫（基隆市）」策劃人。

1983 年（民國 72 年）

· 應「基隆市政府」函聘，擔任「千人寫生比賽」評審委員。

1984 年（民國 73 年）

· 應「臺北市立美術館」邀請，參加慶祝該館開館及藝術家作品聯展。

1985 年（民國 74 年）

· 應「基隆市政府」函聘，擔任「文藝季」評審委員。

· 參加英國倫敦「華威克藝術信託」（Warwick Arts Trust）舉辦「中國現代抽象水墨畫特展」展出。

· 應「臺北市立美術館」邀請，參加「國際水墨畫特展」展出。

· 應黃培珍、荊鴻夫婦邀請，赴美國各地旅遊寫生、參觀美術館與蒐集資料。

· 應「美國在臺協會」邀請，舉行「蕭仁徵遊美水彩寫生畫展」於「美國在臺協會文化中心」展出。

1986 年（民國 75 年）

· 應「臺北市立美術館」邀請，參加「中華民國水墨抽象畫展」展出。

1987 年（民國 76 年）

· 應邀參加第四屆「太平洋國際美術教育會議暨國際美術展覽」，於日本「石川縣立美術館」展出，作品《秋日》為該館典藏。

1988 年（民國 77 年）

· 應「臺灣省立美術館」邀請，參加開館展「中華民國美術發展展覽」展出。

· 彩墨畫作品《夏日山景》為美國「科羅拉多州立大學」典藏。

1989 年（民國 78 年）

· 應「行政院新聞局」函邀，參加「臺北藝術家畫廊畫家作品美、加巡迴展」（於美國、加拿大巡迴展覽兩年），並於首展地點「奧瑞岡大學博物館」擔任作畫示範與講述，作品抽象彩墨畫《互尊》為該博物館典藏。

· 應「中華民國全國美術展覽會」籌備委員會邀請，參加第十二屆「中華民國全國美術展覽會」展出。

· 參加「馬來西亞藝術學院」舉辦「亞洲畫家作品展覽」展出。

1990 年（民國 79 年）

· 應「基隆市立文化中心」邀請，參加「美術家作品展覽」，並被選為資深優秀畫家暨頒獎，作品《夏日松影》為「基隆市文化局」典藏。

· 《藍白點》、《水墨山水》為「國立歷史博物館」典藏。

1992 年（民國 81 年）

· 應「中華民國全國美術展覽會」籌備委員會邀請，參加第十三屆「中華民國全國美術展覽會」展出。

· 應「基隆市立文化中心」邀請，參加「臺灣省北區七縣市第二屆美術家聯展」展出。

· 應「基隆市立文化中心」邀請，舉辦「蕭仁徵、詹碧琴夫婦書畫展」。

1993 年（民國 82 年）

· 抽象水彩畫作品《離別時》、半抽象彩墨畫作品《山醉人醉》為「臺北市立美術館」典藏。

· 應邀參加俄羅斯「聖彼得堡民族博物館」舉行之「中國現代彩墨畫展」暨開幕典禮，並赴東歐各地旅遊寫生、參觀美術館與蒐集資料。

· 應「亞洲水彩畫展」籌備委員會邀請，參加第八屆「亞細亞國際水彩畫展」，於「高雄市中正文化中心」展出。

· 《落日》、《寫意山水》為「國立歷史博物館」典藏。

1994 年（民國 83 年）

· 應「臺灣省立美術館」邀請，參加「中國現代水墨畫大展暨兩岸三地畫家、學者，水墨畫學術研討會」，作品《山水魂》為該館典藏。

· 應甘肅「敦煌研究院」邀請，參加「敦煌國際學術會議」。

1995 年（民國 84 年）

· 參加「中國現代墨彩畫美國巡迴展」，於「國立臺灣藝術教育館」展出。

· 應邀參加「國立臺灣藝術教育館」舉辦之「中華民國第一屆現代水墨畫展」展出。

· 成立「二十一世紀現代水墨畫會」，與劉國松、袁德星、黃朝湖、黃光男等為共同發起人。

· 受聘擔任第十四屆「中華民國全國美術展覽會」評審委員。

· 應「中華民國全國美術展覽會」籌備委員會邀請，參加第十四屆「中華民國全國美術展覽會」展出。

1996 年（民國 85 年）

· 參加「亞太地區水彩畫家作品邀請展覽」，於「國立臺灣藝術教育館」展出。

· 應南京「江蘇省美術館」邀請，參加「二十一世紀現代水墨畫會會員作品展覽」，於該館展出。

· 應「國立國父紀念館」邀請，參加「二十一世紀現代水墨畫會會員作品展覽」，於該館展出。

1997 年（民國 86 年）

· 現代水彩畫作品《牆》為「高雄市立美術館」典藏。

· 應「基隆市立文化中心」邀請，舉辦首屆「藝術薪火傳承：美術家蕭仁徵先生繪畫展覽」，作品《春漲煙嵐》為「基隆市文化局」典藏。

· 「二十一世紀現代水墨畫會」應邀於山東「青島市博物館」、「威海展覽館」與「山東省美術館」等展覽。

1998 年（民國 87 年）

· 「中華民國第二屆現代水墨畫展：21 世紀新展望」於「國立臺灣藝術教育館」展出。

· 參加「臺中市立文化中心」15 周年館慶，於該文化中心舉辦之「全國水墨畫邀請展」展出。

· 應「中華民國全國美術展覽會」籌備委員會邀請，參加第十五屆「中華民國全國美術展覽會」展出。

1999 年（民國 88 年）

· 參加「跨世紀亞太水彩畫展」，於「國立臺灣藝術教育館」展出。

· 參加「臺灣現代水墨畫展」，作品《秋水篇》於比利時布魯塞爾展出。

2000 年（民國 89 年）

· 參加「臺灣現代水墨畫大展」，於四川「成都現代美術館」、北京「中國美術館」展出。

· 參加「庚辰龍年名家創作特展」，於「國立臺灣藝術教育館」展出。

· 參加「中國當代水墨新貌展」，於「國立臺灣藝術教育館」展出。

2001 年（民國 90 年）

· 參加「新世紀亞太水彩畫邀請展」，於「國立臺灣藝術教育館」展出。

· 參加「水墨新動向」展，於「高雄市立中正文化中心」展出。

· 應「誠品書店」邀請，於其基隆店三樓藝文空間舉辦「彩墨交融協奏曲」個人畫展。

2002 年（民國 91 年）

· 應「陝西歷史博物館」邀請，與夫人詹碧琴於該館舉辦聯展，畫作《冬雀》為該館典藏。

· 參加「臺中市政府文化局」舉辦「全國彩墨藝術大展」展出。

· 參加「水墨新紀元：當代水墨畫兩岸交流展」，於「國立國父紀念館」展出。

2003 年（民國 92 年）

· 參加「國際彩墨布旗藝術展」，於臺灣、美國、法國、波蘭、馬來西亞等國巡迴展出。

· 參加「臺灣美術戰後五十年作品展」，於臺北市「長流美術館」展出。

2004 年（民國 93 年）

· 參加「臺中市政府文化局」舉辦「全國彩墨藝術大展」展出。

· 參加「水墨新動向」展，並分別於「國立成功大學」、「逢甲大學」與山東「青島市文化博覽中心」、四川「成都現代藝術館」、「九寨溝博物館」等多處巡迴展出。

2005 年（民國 94 年）

· 參加「臺中市政府文化局」舉辦「國際彩墨衣裳藝術大展」展出。

2006 年（民國 95 年）

· 參加「臺灣國際水彩畫協會會員聯展」，於「國立國父紀念館」展出。

· 參加「水墨變相：現代水墨在臺灣」展，於「臺北市立美術館」展出。

· 參加「臺中市政府文化局」舉辦「國際彩墨方巾藝術大展」展出。

2007 年（民國 96 年）

· 成立「基隆海藍水彩畫會」，並擔任該會之創會會長。

· 參加「臺中市政府文化局」舉辦「國際彩墨圖騰藝術大展」展出。

· 參加「臺北縣政府文化局」舉辦「臺灣國際水彩畫邀請展」展出。

· 參加「成都現代雙年展：水墨新動向－臺灣現代水墨畫展」，於四川「成都現代藝術館」展出。

2008 年（民國 97 年）

· 參加「臺中市政府文化局」舉辦「國際彩墨生態藝術大展」展出。

· 參加「國際彩墨圖騰藝術西班牙展」，於西班牙「O＋O 國際藝術交流中心」展出。

· 參加「臺灣國際水彩畫邀請展」，於「國立中正紀念堂」展出。

2009 年（民國 98 年）

- 參加「臺中市政府文化局」舉辦「國際彩墨塗雅藝術大展」展出。
- 應「研華文教基金會」邀請，「基隆海藍水彩畫會聯展」於臺北市「研華公益藝廊」展出。
- 成立「新東方現代書畫家協會」，為該協會之發起人。

2010 年（民國 99 年）

- 參加「臺中市政府文化局」舉辦「國際彩墨人文藝術大展」展出。
- 「新東方現代書畫家協會」首屆展覽，於「基隆市立文化中心」展出。
- 參加第三屆「傳統與現代」當代華人水墨書法創作邀請展，於河南省鄭州市展出。

2011 年（民國 100 年）

- 參加「臺中市政府文化局」舉辦「國際彩墨扇子藝術大展」展出。
- 參加「基隆海藍水彩畫會展」，於「基隆市立文化中心」展出。
- 參加「新東方現代書畫會會員聯展」，於「基隆市立文化中心」展出。

2012 年（民國 101 年）

- 參加「臺中市政府文化局」舉辦「國際彩墨面具藝術大展」展出。
- 參加「基隆海藍水彩畫會展」，於「基隆市立文化中心」展出。
- 參加「新東方現代書畫會會員聯展」，於「基隆市立文化中心」展出。
- 參加「佛光山佛陀紀念館」舉辦之「百畫齊芳—百位藝術家畫佛館特展」，並捐贈水墨壓克力彩作品《星雲佛光圖》予該館典藏。

2013 年（民國 102 年）

- 參加「臺中市政府文化局」舉辦「國際彩墨帽子藝術大展」展出。
- 參加「基隆海藍水彩畫會展」，於「基隆市立文化中心」展出。
- 參加「新東方現代書畫會會員聯展」，於「基隆市立文化中心」展出。

2014 年（民國 103 年）

- 參加「臺中市政府文化局」舉辦「國際彩墨鞋子藝術大展」展出。
- 參加「基隆海藍水彩畫會展」，於「基隆市立文化中心」展出。
- 參加「新東方現代書畫會會員聯展」，於「基隆市立文化中心」展出。
- 參加「臺灣五十現代水墨畫展」開幕展，於臺北市「築空間」展出。

2015 年（民國 104 年）

- 參加「臺中市政府文化局」舉辦「國際彩墨蝴蝶藝術大展」展出。
- 參加「基隆海藍水彩畫會展」，於「基隆市立文化中心」展出。

· 參加「基隆藝術家聯盟交流協會聯展」，於「基隆市立文化中心」展出。

· 參加「新東方現代書畫會會員聯展」，於「基隆市立文化中心」展出。

· 參加「絲路翰墨情」兩岸四地書畫名家邀請展，於「香港國際創價學會」展出。

· 作品《昇》、《雨中樹》為「國立臺灣美術館」典藏。

2016 年（民國 105 年）

· 參加「臺中市政府文化局」舉辦「國際彩墨魚類藝術大展」展出。

· 參加「基隆海藍水彩畫會展」，於「基隆市立文化中心」展出。

· 參加「基隆藝術家聯盟交流協會聯展」，於「基隆市立文化中心」展出。

· 參加「新東方現代書畫會會員聯展」，於「基隆市立文化中心」展出。

2017 年（民國 106 年）

· 參加「臺中市政府文化局」舉辦「國際彩墨花與城市藝術大展」展出。

· 參加「基隆海藍水彩畫會展」，於「基隆市立文化中心」展出。

· 參加「基隆藝術家聯盟交流協會聯展」，於「基隆市立文化中心」展出。

· 參加「新東方現代書畫會會員聯展」，於「基隆市立文化中心」展出。

2018 年（民國 107 年）

· 參加「臺中市政府文化局」舉辦「國際彩墨花花世界藝術大展」展出。

· 參加「基隆海藍水彩畫會展」，於「基隆市立文化中心」展出。

· 參加「基隆藝術家聯盟交流協會聯展」，於「基隆市立文化中心」展出。

· 參加「新東方現代書畫會會員聯展」，於「基隆市立文化中心」展出。

2019 年（民國 108 年）

· 參加「臺中市政府文化局」舉辦「國際彩墨鳥類藝術大展」展出。

· 參加「基隆海藍水彩畫會展」，於「基隆市立文化中心」展出。

· 參加「基隆藝術家聯盟交流協會聯展」，於「基隆市立文化中心」展出。

· 參加「新東方現代書畫會會員聯展」，於「基隆市立文化中心」展出。

2020 年（民國 109 年）

· 參加「有意味的形式」，於「基隆市立文化中心」展出。

2021 年（民國 110 年）

· 個展「墨動─蕭仁徵現代畫開拓展」，於「國立臺灣師範大學美術系德群藝廊」展出。

國家圖書館出版品預行編目資料

墨動：蕭仁徵現代畫開拓展 = Ink Movement : Xiao Jen-
Cheng and the Expansion of Modern Painting / 江桂珍主
編 . -- 初版 . -- 臺北市：國立歷史博物館，民 110.11
　　面；　公分
ISBN 978-986-532-434-6（平裝）
1. 書畫　2. 作品集
941.5　　　　　　　　　　　　　　　110017656

蕭仁徵
現代畫開拓展

墨動

Ink Movement
Hsiao Jen-cheng and the Expansion of Modern Painting

發 行 人	廖新田	Publisher	Liao Hsin-tien
出 版 者	國立歷史博物館	Commissioner	National Museum of History
	10055 臺北市徐州路 21 號		21, Xuzhou Road, Taipei 10055, R.O.C.
	電話：+886-2-23610270		Tel : +886-2-23610270
	傳真：+886-2-23931771		Fax: +886-2-23931771
	網站：www.nmh.gov.tw		www.nmh.gov.tw
編　　輯	國立歷史博物館編輯委員會	Editorial Committee	Editorial Committee of National Museum of History
主　　編	江桂珍	Curator · Chief Editor	Chiang Kuei-chen
執行編輯	郭沛一、陳奕安	Executive Editors	Guo Pei-yi, Chen Yi-an
策　　展	郭沛一	Curator	Guo Pei-yi
英文翻譯	萬象翻譯	Translator	Linguitronics Co. Ltd.
英文審稿	廣燕心	English Proofreader	Kayleigh Madjar
美術設計	顧佩綺	Art Designs	Koo Pei-chi
總　　務	許志榮	Chief General Affairs	Hsu Chih-jung
主　　計	徐素芬	Chief Accountant	Hsu Su-fen
製版印刷	四海圖文傳播股份有限公司	Printer	Suhai Design and Printing Company
	23585 新北市中和區錦和路 28 號 3 樓		3F, No. 28, Jinho Rd., Zhonghe Dist., New Taipei City, Taiwan,
	電話：+886-2-27618117		R.O.C. 23585
			Tel: +886-2-2761-8117
出版日期	中華民國 110 年 11 月	Publication Date	November 2021
版　　次	初版	Edition	First Edition
其他類型版本說明：本書無其他類型版本		Other Edition	None for This Edition
定　　價	新臺幣 880 元	Price	NT$ 880
展 售 處	五南文化廣場台中總店	Museum Shop	Wunanbooks
	40042 臺中市中山路 6 號		6, Chung Shan Rd., Taichung, Taiwan , R.O.C. 40042
	電話：+886-4-22260330		Tel: +886-4-22260330
	國家書店松江門市		Songjiang Department of Government Bookstore
	10485 臺北市松江路 209 號 1 樓		209, Songjiang Rd., Taipei, Taiwan , R.O.C. 10485
	電話：+886-2-25180207		Tel: +886-2-25180207
	國家網路書店		Government Online Bookstore
	http://www.govbooks.com.tw		http:// www.govbooks.com.tw
統一編號	1011001697	GPN	1011001697
國際書號	978-986-532-434-6	ISBN	978-986-532-434-6